Fiction

Feast!

Lau~~ri~~ rint
jour~~nal~~ She
is currently employed as a commissioning editor with The
Women's Press in London. She is the co-editor of
Something to Savour: Food for Thought from Women Writers
(The Women's Press, 1996), editor of *A Glimpse of Green:
Women Writing on Gardens* (The Women's Press, 1996), and
edits The Women's Press young adult series, Livewire.

Helen Windrath is senior commissioning editor and
rights manager at The Women's Press. Prior to this she
worked for Commonword, a north-west community
publisher, based in Manchester. She also edited *The
Women's Press Book of New Myth and Magic* (The Women's
Press, 1993) and *Reader, I Murdered Him, Too* (The
Women's Press, 1995). She lives in London.

Also edited by Laurie Critchley and Helen Windrath from The Women's Press:

The Women's Press Book of New Myth and Magic (1993)
ed Helen Windrath

Reader, I Murdered Him, Too (1995) ed Helen Windrath

Something to Savour: Food for Thought from Women Writers (1996) eds Laurie Critchley and Helen Windrath

A Glimpse of Green: Women Writing on Gardens (1996) ed Laurie Critchley

Feast!

WOMEN WRITE ABOUT FOOD

LAURIE CRITCHLEY AND
HELEN WINDRATH, EDITORS

First published by The Women's Press Ltd, 1996
A member of the Namara Group
34 Great Sutton Street, London EC1V 0DX

British Library Cataloguing-in-Publication Data
A catalogue record for this book is available from the British Library

ISBN 0 7043 4500 5

Typeset in Bembo by The Harrington Consultancy
Printed and bound in Great Britain by BPC Paperbacks Ltd

Permissions

The Women's Press would like to thank the following:

Aunt Lute Books and Virago for permission to reprint 'Hot Chicken Wings' by Jyl Lynn Felman © 1992.

Susan Bergholz Literary Services, New York, for permission to reprint 'Crawfish Love' from *Loverboys*. Copyright © Ana Castillo 1996. All rights reserved.

Ellen Galford for permission to reprint an extract from *The Fires of Bride*, 1986.

Githa Hariharan, care of David Godwin, for permission to reprint 'The Remains of the Feast'.

HarperCollins *Publishers* Ltd for permission to reprint an extract from *Anita and Me* by Meera Syal, 1996.

Andrea Levy, care of David Grossman, for permission to reprint 'The Meatballs' from *Every Light in the House Burnin'*, 1994.

Macmillan Canada for permission to reprint 'Mangiamania' from *Urban Scrawl* by Erika Ritter, 1984.

Val McDermid, care of Gregory and Radice, for permission to reprint 'Breathtaking Ignorance'.

NeWest Press for permission to reprint an extract from *Chorus of Mushrooms* by Hiromi Goto, 1994.

Lesléa Newman for permission to reprint 'Red, White and Absolutely Blue' from *Every Woman's Dream*, published by New Victoria Publishers, Norwich, Vermont, USA. Copyright © Lesléa Newman 1994.

Mei Ng for permission to reprint 'This Early' from *Tasting Life Twice*, edited by E J Levy, 1995.

M Nourbese Philip for permission to reprint 'Burn Sugar'.

Michèle Roberts, care of Aitken & Stone, for permission to reprint an extract from *A Piece of the Night*, 1978.

Kathleen Tyau, care of The Peters Fraser & Dunlop Group, for permission to reprint an extract from *A Little Too Much Is Enough*, 1995.

Virago and Random House US for permission to reprint an extract from *Gather Together in My Name* by Maya Angelou, 1985.

Contents

From Chorus of Mushrooms

Hiromi Goto

Tinkle tinkle of door ... I stood in the doorway and breathed in deep the scent of spices foreign to my senses. I was bemused.

'Hello, you must be Sam Tonkatsu's daughter, I can see the family resemblance, nice to meet you.' She stood firm and solid behind the cash register, wearing a white apron that covered her from neck to mid-thigh. Her head perched on top like a snow woman. She smiled hugely, and her teeth were comfortably crooked.

'Hi,' I said, and kind of waved, for the lack of anything better to do. I was shocked. Dad came here? To this store?

'How's your Dad doing? I haven't seen him come around for a couple of weeks now. He must be getting low on his salted seaweed paste.'

'Dad eats salted seaweed paste?' my mouth dropped open.

'Funny guy, your Dad. Never says much and all he ever buys is salted seaweed paste. Try some pickled radish, I tell him. Try some of our specialty *rāmen*, I say. But no, all he ever buys is the seaweed.'

'Did my Mom come here too?' I asked, starting to doubt the things a saw with my eyes, heard with my ears, as truth. 'Did she ever buy anything too?'

'Not that I know of. Didn't even know Sam had a daughter until I saw you walk in the door. But you couldn't be anyone else. You like he would have looked when he was younger, only with a wig.'

'Gee, thanks a lot. That's very descriptive.'

'Wa! ha! ha! haaa!' she laughed enormously. 'That wasn't meant as an insult, dear! He's quite a striking man, and you're an interesting looking girl.'

'Oh good, this gets better and better.'

'Wa! ha! ha! haaa! Is there anything I can help you with?'

'Yeah, actually. I have a list here, somewhere.' I patted my back pocket and pulled out a folded piece of foolscap.

miso	takuwan
katsuobushi	shōga
wakame	tōfu
konbu	hakusai
mirin	daikon
nori	shōyu
nattō	furikake
yamaimo	satoimo
samma	aji no hiraki
ika	tonkatsu sauce
kome	rāmen

'That's some list,' she said, peering over my shoulder and breathing quite heavily into my hair. 'Run out of the staples, huh?'

'I wouldn't know. My Obāchan* gave me the list, and I know what the words mean, but I have no idea what they are.'

'Isn't that some sort of aphasia? Were you in an accident or something? Maybe it's personal, huh. Tell me if I'm being too pushy.'

'Pardon?' There were too many things swirling in my head.

'Never mind, I'll help you out.'

'By the way,' something occurred to me. 'The *tonkatsu* in *tonkatsu* sauce?'

'Yes?'

'Is that the same *tonkatsu* like my name?'

'You mean you don't know?' She was amazed.

'No, I guess I don't.' I felt my face glow warmer, but I had to know.

'Maybe you should ask your Dad,' she said, shooting price stickers on the bottom of a few cans, glancing up at my face between every tha–chunk. 'I'm not sure of the origins and such. It could have a totally different character spelling. Or it could be a nickname that turned into a real name.'

'I don't know if he remembers. Please tell me. I want to know now.' I was so close to a different understanding, I could almost taste it.

'Well, the only *tonkatsu* I'm familiar with is a food.'

'Oh boy,' I muttered, 'I don't know if I can stand another shock.'

'It's a type of breaded deep-fried pork cutlet.'

'Ohmygod.'

---

* [grandmother]

'I think it's very unique and interesting. Maybe your father's family was in the food or restaurant business. Who knows, maybe his family invented them!' she expanded, warming to the subject.

'I can't stand it.'

'There's nothing nicer than a *tonkatsu* dinner on a cold winter evening. It fills you up and everyone eats them licketysplit. Everyone loves *tonkatsu*. Don't tell me you've never had one.'

'I've never had one.'

'Well!' she said, outraged, 'well, it just won't do!' She bustled to the meagre book and magazine rack and flipped through a stack. Chose a thin, colour photo recipe book of Japanese food and smacked it against her thigh. Dust flew and made me sneeze twice.

'Take this. On the house. You learn how to make *tonkatsu* and you eat them up. Make your Obāchan proud of you.'

'Thanks!' I flipped through the pages, the photographs making my mouth water for things I'd never tasted.

'Put that down for now,' she said. 'I'll show you what you've got on that shopping list of yours.'

I tagged after her, pushing a shopping cart. Pausing in front of the small produce section, and pointing to certain vegetables, she said the words aloud.

'Daikon.' *Big white radish thing as long as my forearm.*

'Hakusai.' *Leafy frilly cabbage thing I've seen in Safeway.*

'Shōga.' *Fresh root of ginger, translation not literal.*

'Satoimo.' *Little fur-covered balls, root vegetable, no tuber.*

'Don't worry, once you eat what they are, you won't forget them,' she swept through the aisles, dropping items into the shopping cart.

'*Mirin, nori, miso.* ... The recipe book should help. Is your mom white?'

No, she just doesn't make Japanese food.'

'Oh, that's too bad. Eating's a part of being after all. How many pound of rice do you want?'

'Oh, just a couple for now, I guess.'

'They only come in twenty-five or fifty pound bags.'

'Oh,' I said blushing, embarrassed of my ignorance. 'The twenty-five pound bag, then. What was it you said my Dad bought all the time?'

'Salted seaweed paste. Excellent on hot rice.'

'I'll have some of that too.'

'Okay. I think that about covers your list.' She started ringing it through the till. I was overwhelmed. The strange but familiar food. Dad and his seaweed. Our name.

'That'll be $187.49.'

'Good God!'

'It gets pricey. Most of it's imported you know. Can't be helped. Did you bring enough money?'

'I was going to treat myself to a movie and maybe a new pair of jeans, but I guess that's out.'

'You can put some stuff back if you want,' she raised her heavy eyebrows. 'I don't mind ringing it through the till again, we're not so busy.'

'Nah, it's all right. I should go home before it gets dark, anyway.'

'Here's your change. Let me help you out to your car.' She swung the sack of rice over one shoulder and clutched a box beneath her other arm. The door tinkle tinkled. I popped open the trunk and set my box inside. As the woman put down the rice, I asked,

'What's your name anyway?'

'Sushi.'

Nothing could surprise me now. I stuck out my hand.

'Thanks for all your help, Sushi.'

She shook my hand briskly and rattled my head in the process.

'Tell me how the *tonkatsu* works out.'

From *Chorus of Mushrooms*, published by The Women's Press

A Little Too Much Is Enough

Kathleen Tyau

All day long I starved myself, but before we left for the wedding I sat at the kitchen table and watched my father eat saimin. I sat so close to him the steam from the hot broth made my eyes water.

'Get a bowl,' he said.

I shook my head. I was determined to save my stomach for dinner that night. I knew the food would be good. My cousin Beetle Wong was getting married, and his parents were relieved that he was marrying Chinese. And not just any old Chinese. Beetle had met Teena Lum-Tong while cruising Kahala Mall, where the rich girls shop. Three hundred fifty relatives and friends were celebrating at a Chinese nine-course dinner in Waikiki after the wedding.

My father says the noodles sop up the alcohol and keep him from getting drunk. When my mother said, 'Better eat another bowl of saimin, Kuhio,' I knew they were preparing for a long night of drinking with the uncles.

At the entrance to the Hilton banquet hall I checked the guest list for my name. When I discovered I was sitting with the older cousins, I nearly cartwheeled across the room. At fourteen I had finally graduated from the children's table.

The oldest one at my table was Frankel Choy, a cousin from my mother's side. And his wife, Wei Ling, six months hapai. My brother Buzzy. The twins, Sue-Sue and Sam. My cousin Rhoda Chew, who everybody calls Tookie. Tookie was two years older than me so I always got stuck wearing her hand-me-downs. Finally I came to his name. Robert Michelangelo Wong. My second cousin Bobby. Nobody told me he was coming home. Our fathers were cousins, which meant we saw each other only at big parties now, at funerals or weddings.

Bobby wasn't tough to spot in the crowded room. He played guard for Oregon State on a basketball scholarship. Even sitting, he was a grasshopper in a swarm of ants. All legs.

I forced myself not to run to the table. I pulled out my chair like it was my mother's good china. Buzzy was already there, trading elephant jokes with Sue-Sue and Sam. I ignored him. Pretended I didn't see Bobby at first.

'Hi, Frankel,' I said. 'Hi, Wei Ling. Is the baby kicking yet?' I pointed at her stomach, which still looked smaller than mine. Not waiting for an answer, I turned to Bobby. 'Aay, Bobby, howzit? Teaching them haoles how to play ball?'

Bobby greeted me by standing up, unlike the other boy cousins, who slouched deeper in their chairs. I liked the way he had to look down at me.

'Hey, Mahealani,' he said softly. 'How you doing, kid? Long time no see.' He leaned over and squeezed my shoulder. I reached up for his hand. Too late. Wished I could say hello all over again, cut the pidgin, call him Robert Michelangelo, like I wrote in my diary.

Even though we were five years apart in age, Bobby and I always ended up playing together when our families met for picnics and potluck suppers back when we were kids. We played kickball, sky inning, doctor and nurse. The day I told him I was never getting married, he let me be the doctor. Let me feel his forehead, take his pulse, perform the operation that saved his life. Then one day, while we were playing in the empty lot next to the sugar-cane fields, I saw Bobby make shi-shi behind a boulder. I only saw him from the back, and I didn't see anything, because he kept his pants on, but my legs felt weak. When he came back to play with me, he threw me a sky ball and said, 'Try catch this one.' But I let the ball fall behind the keawe bushes and spent a long time crawling around in the dirt pretending I was looking for it.

I don't know how Tookie managed to get the seat next to Bobby. She must have switched her placecard with mine so she could moon all over him. I never should have told her how I felt about him. Once she knew, she didn't stop plotting.

'I'm going to Oregon State too,' she had said. 'Bobby will still be around when I get there.'

'Forget it, Rhoda.' She hated when I called her that. 'You'll never pass the test.' But deep down inside I was worried. I had to get to Oregon before she did.

She wore too much mascara that evening and her lipstick was smeared, but of course I didn't tell her. I couldn't keep my eyes off her dress. It was a body-hugging cheongsam with a long slit up the side, her mother's dress, and it was red, like mine, except that my dress had a loose, dropped waist, so I could eat without having to suck in my stomach. I knew everyone would look at her and then at me and then back at her again. At least her dress was too big in the bust and too tight in the hips, so the wrong parts of Tookie showed.

I decided to play it cool. Bobby had once said to me, 'The thing I like about you, Mahi, is you aren't silly.' Tookie talked too much and snorted like a baby pig when she laughed. I figured she would drive Bobby nuts after a while, and when the band started playing, he'd come to me to escape. I took my place between the twins, Sue-Sue and Sam.

Then Uncle Joey came over and made one of the twins switch tables with him. The aunties and uncles called Joey 'Small Uncle' because he was the youngest, not because of his size. Next to him, everyone else in the family looked like termites.

'That's right,' said Uncle Wing. 'Go and sit with the kids. More food for us.' The aunties laughed. Buzzy and I and the cousins at my table groaned. Nobody wanted Uncle Joey at their table, because he dug around for the best pieces of meat and messed up the serving dish. Then he ate so fast everyone at his table had to eat faster to keep up.

'No, no, go back,' said Tookie, but it was too late.

'I think I'll go help out the kids too,' said Aunty Nona, making her way to our table.

'Oh no. That's all we need,' I said. 'Why do we have to get stuck with both of them?'

'Shhh, they'll hear you,' said Wei Ling, who clearly was not related to any of us.

The other twin moved to the table with the big eaters, which left me with Uncle Joey on one side and Aunty Nona on the other. My father said Aunty Nona was bossy because she should have been a teacher but sold crackseed instead. But my mother disagreed. She said, 'Nona means well. She has a good heart. She just loves to eat.'

That night, as Aunty Nona sat down next to me, I

prayed I wasn't the one at the table she was goodhearted enough to boss. She looked like a Christmas gift in her long white muumuu with the big red hibiscus print. She grinned at me.

'How lucky,' she said. 'I get to sit by my favourite niece.'

'Oh, Aunty,' I said, trying not to wince as she pinched my arm. 'I'm so glad you came to sit with us.' I didn't want Bobby to think I was a whiner.

Uncle Joey banged his water glass with a spoon, signalling for a toast. I poured tea in my cup and wondered how I could get someone to slip me some Scotch. Uncle Joey raised his jigger in the direction of the newlyweds, Beetle and Teena.

'Here's to you two,' he said. 'If you two no love we too as much as we love you two, then here's to we all.'

He had borrowed that toast from somebody else's wedding, but I loved it anyway. I could repeat it in my sleep, because he gave the same toast at every family wedding. Sometimes I lay awake at night trying to figure out where the t-o's and t-o-o's and t-w-o's belonged. I asked him once, but he looked worried that I might steal his lines.

We knocked our glasses together, Beetle kissed Teena, Frankel kissed Wei Ling's baby finger, and Tookie and I sighed at the same time. Aunty Hannah Mele sang the blessing in Hawaiian, and finally, eons after my father's bowls of saimin, out came the food.

The waiters marched into the hall carrying enormous platters of cold steamed chicken covered with chopped ginger, green onions, oil, and sprigs of Chinese parsley. Everyone clapped and started eating. Except for our table.

'Wait,' said Aunty Nona, digging in her handbag for her Brownie box camera. 'Let Aunty take a picture first.'

'Oh, Aunty, not now,' said Buzzy.

'Now look this way and smile, everybody,' she said. 'Tookie, don't slouch. Bobby, move a little bit so Aunty can get all of the chicken. That's good. Mahi, don't play with your chopsticks.'

'Oh, for crying out loud,' said Uncle Joey. 'Just take the picture so we can eat.'

'Just one picture,' she said. 'While the food still looks good.'

He should have known it didn't do any good to complain. At every nine-course dinner, as far back as I can remember, Aunty Nona waited until the food came out and we were ready to dive in. Then she'd make us wait while she took a picture. In all her photos, our heads are chopped off, but the food looks great.

One small click at last, then another just to be sure, and then we grabbed our chopsticks and the real clicking began.

'I can help myself,' I said to Aunty Nona, who was piling chicken on my plate.

'Here's another good piece,' she said, sticking her elbow in my face. She transferred a piece of chicken from her plate to mine as if doing me a favour. According to tribal law, I owed her the duty of eating it.

'No no, Aunty,' I protested. 'Please. I have enough. I won't be able to eat what's coming.'

'Don't worry,' she said. 'Take your time. You have all night. Besides, you're still young and skinny. You don't have to watch your weight like me.' She laughed. Only when she was trying to feed me did I suddenly become too skinny. I leaned against her elbow, but she leaned back harder and the chicken thigh fell on my plate.

I hoped my favourite dish, the oyster rolls, would come out before I was stuffed. When Aunty Nona wasn't looking, I slipped the chicken thigh onto Uncle Joey's plate. I knew if I ate slowly, the food on our table would be gone before Aunty Nona could feed me more.

I looked around the room. Everyone seemed to be talking and eating at the same time. The voices, chopsticks, and bowls sounded like sand and gravel in a cement mixer.

Soon the chicken was gone. Frankel proclaimed the empty platter was to be used for the bones. We passed the plate around. Uncle Joey put the dish of bones down in front of me.

'Why did you put it by me?'

'I thought you were on a diet,' he said. 'Just shut up and eat.'

'We forgot to toast the chicken,' Tookie cried. Uncle Joey poured Scotch from the bottle on the table. I stuck out my empty jigger, which Aunty Nona filled with tea.

'To the chicken.'

'To the chicken.'

'To the chicken bones.'

Now the hot dishes were coming out fast, along with small hills of steamed rice. Roast duck with crispy red skin. Shrimp and crab on mounds of vegetables. Shiny black mushrooms, elephant ear fungus, bamboo shoots, and thick slices of abalone. Beetle's parents were going whole hog. I knew the food wouldn't run out. In fact, we would not be able to eat it all. If we did, Uncle Danny and Aunty Ah Oi would be disgraced because they hadn't ordered enough food. Sometimes I think the real purpose of the nine-course dinner is to show everyone that there will always be enough, that we will always have more than we really need. Uncle Joey, Aunty Nona, my father Kuhio – my whole family – would never tolerate a life of restraint, of just getting by.

The oyster rolls came out at last. I forked up two, even though I only had room for one. Aunty Nona put another roll on my plate. The oyster rolls were crispy on the outside, but when I bit into one, the juice oozed out and dribbled down my chin.

I watched Bobby eat. He caught my eye but didn't say anything, just winked. Tookie glared at me. I looked at my plate. I was beginning to feel like maybe I still had a chance.

I once wrote Bobby a letter that said, 'Dear Bobby, I saw you making shi-shi in the empty lot. But I still love you. Get chance?' Before I could give him the letter, my mother found it and asked me what we'd been doing. I didn't see Bobby much after that, and then he was off to Oregon.

The waiter took away the plate of bones. I looked up and saw my father with his arm around Uncle Wing. My father's cheeks were red his necktie was crooked. My mother sat talking to Aunty Lucy, but I knew she was keeping an eye on him. He and my uncle staggered across the room to toast the married couple. Two other uncles joined them in front of the head table.

'Goon bui! Goon bui! Pak til dow lau!' they shouted, and swigged and swayed.

After the oyster rolls came intermission. That was our chance to walk around and make room for more food. The MC, Uncle Danny's best friend in the army, introduced the relatives and guests who had come from the mainland. Bobby, of course, the basketball star. Aunty Lucy, but Uncle Chin stayed in Sacramento because he hates to fly. A cousin and his wife from LA on their honeymoon. Nobody could figure out why they came *here* when they lived next door to Disneyland, where Beetle and Teena were going for *their* honeymoon. An aunty and uncle from Michigan. Their daughter, Cassandra, whom nobody recognised at first.

'Cleopatra's certainly filled out,' whispered Aunty Nona.

'Her name is Cassandra,' I said.

'Must be the air from the Great Lakes,' said my aunty. 'The cold air makes the fat form on your chi-chis.' She stuffed a large black mushroom into her mouth, whole.

Even Bobby turned around to stare. I contemplated the last oyster roll, lonely on the serving dish.

Shark-fin soup followed the intermission. Frankel served the soup, since he was the oldest male cousin. By right, Uncle Joey should have served, but he declined.

'I need time to eat,' he said, refusing to take the ladle. Wei Ling held Frankel's necktie back so it didn't fall in the soup.

'Pass me your bowl,' Frankel said to me. 'Kiddies first.' I wanted to wrap the tie around his neck.

After the soup came bowls of white steamed buns and thick, fatty slices of stewed red pork.

'This dish means long life,' said Aunty Nona.

'No, it's red, red for good luck,' said Frankel.

'Maybe Beetle and Teena will find gold in Disneyland,' said Uncle Joey.

Long life, luck, money, a house full of children – no one at our table could agree. Everybody had an answer, but I knew if I pointed at the Chinese characters on top of a birthday cake, or at the sign over the entranceway to the restaurant, I would get the same responses. We were Chinese, but Hawaiian – and now Americans, able to vote – and many of us could not read or speak Chinese of any dialect. For all we knew, the Chinese words on the cake and over the door said, 'May your teeth rot from all this sugar,' or, 'You are crazy to eat here.' My family ignored such possibilities, content with thinking they were blessed with luck and every other bit of good fortune they could imagine.

I searched for a small piece of pork. I bit off the fat and spit it on my plate. Aunty Nona jabbed me with her elbow.

'That's the best part,' she said.

'You can have it,' I replied.

'Let's see if I can find you a better piece,' she said, poking around the bowl.

I don't remember what course came next. I had lost count. All I knew was that I'd eaten too much and still had a long way to go. Even with Uncle Joey and Aunty Nona helping us out, we lagged behind the tables of big-eating adults. One of the uncles came over to our table and took away a platter to help us out. The bottle of Scotch was nearly empty, but we were behind in that too. The uncles at the next table were on their third or fourth bottle. We tried to catch up by toasting the rice, the waiters, the shoyu, the mustard.

Finally, we were done. Frankel let out his belt buckle two notches. Bobby loosened his necktie. His hair fell across his eyes like it did when we were kids playing in the empty lot next to the sugar-cane fields. I stared at his hands. I thought about how we played the piano together in the red dirt, his fingers running over mine. About my sweaty palms searching for the beat on his bony chest. About the cotton sunsuits I wore, the spaghetti straps that sometimes came undone. Once, I caught him staring, and when I looked down and saw my bare chi-chis, I grabbed the front of my dress and ran home. I knew I should tell him I had changed my mind about getting married, so he wouldn't fall in love with Tookie or a haole girl from Oregon. He'd only have to wait a few years. I'd tell him later, when the lights were turned down and the music started and he asked me to dance.

'Look, Mahi, you spilled gravy all over your nice dress,'

Aunty Nona said to me. 'I told you to open your napkin up all the way.'

I rubbed at the spot with a napkin dipped in water, trying not to make it look like I had gone to the bathroom down there. Another platter full of bones sat in front of me. Buzzy stirred the bones and fat and gravy into slop.

'Stop that. Stop that right now,' said Aunty Nona. 'Take away the bones,' she said to the waiter. 'And bring us some boxes for the leftovers.' She bustled over to the younger children's table to gather up their half-eaten platters of food.

I scrubbed furiously and blew on the spot, trying to evaporate the stain now spreading wider and wider across the front of my dress. The band was tuning up, but my father was already dancing with a red-faced Beetle. Nine courses plus two bowls of saimin weren't enough to keep my father down. My mother had folded up all the dirty napkins at her table, and Aunty Lucy was doing most of the talking now. Tookie, Rhoda, the slut, was stroking Bobby's sleeve and whispering something to him. Her lips touched his ear now and then. Uncle Joey leaned back in his chair and belched. Beetle finally broke free of my father and ran to give his new wife, Teena Lum-Tong Wong, a long, hard kiss, as if he were afraid she would disappear.

From *A Little Too Much Is Enough*, published by The Women's Press

The Meatballs

Andrea Levy

My mum went away to an Open University summer school. She gave us good warning that she would be going. I'd known for about a year. But it still seemed to come as a bit of a shock to my dad.

'Oh, you going so soon?' he asked.

'I told you from a long time, Dad,' my mum protested.

'Yes, but I didn't realise it was so soon.'

My mum gave instructions for most household chores and appointed someone to each task.

'And Dad,' she said, 'I've left some meatballs in the kitchen. They just need frying up to heat them through – they should be all right.'

At tea-time an acrid smell began to envelop the flat. I went into the kitchen. My dad was standing over the stove, as smoke wafted up all around him. I'd never seen him cook before. He was pushing at something in a frying pan, jabbing it like he was trying to kill it over again.

'What's that smell, Dad?' I asked.

'Meatballs,' he said.

He looked intently at the pan. There were three plates to the side of the cooker. Each one had three boiled potatoes and a small pile of peas on it.

'What's for tea, Dad?' I said, hoping it was something else.

'Meatballs,' he said.

'They smell a bit funny Dad,' I said.

'Cha,' he said, turning and scowling at me. 'Get out from under my feet.' So I left the kitchen.

'What's that smell?' my brother asked.

'Meatballs,' I repeated.

'They pong,' he said. I shrugged.

My dad came in from the kitchen and lifted up the flap in the table. We never ate at this table when my mum was around. We always ate balancing the plates on our lap and watching the television. But there was only my dad, my brother and me and the difference meant that everything changed. My dad threw down a bundle of cutlery on to the table.

'Come Angela, put on the knives and forks.'

I laid them out as best I could on the tiny table — it was hard to fit three sets on and have enough room for you to move your arms.

My dad came in again carrying a bowl filled with tinned peaches. He set them down in the middle of the table and smiled at me. 'They're for afters, if you eat everything up.'

I looked at my brother and we rolled our eyes. Then my dad came in with the three plates. The meatballs were steaming hot and with the steam came an awful stench of rotting flesh.

'Dad, those meatballs don't smell right,' I said. My

brother stuck his nose over his and pulled a face. We sat at the table.

'Come – eat up,' my dad said.

I looked at my brother then cut into the now-cold potatoes. My brother's mouth was still curled up at the edges.

'Come – eat!' my dad insisted. As he did a pea shot out from his mouth and landed in the bowl of tinned peaches. I watched it shoot out and land with an audible plop right in the centre of the bowl. My dad looked at the pea, quickly removed it and put it back in his mouth. Then he cut into one of his meatballs and the smell wafted up to him. 'Oh dear,' he said. 'I don't think these are right.'

'I feel sick,' my brother said, pushing his plate away.

'Well, just eat up your peas and potato nuh.'

My brother and I sat back from the table and folded our arms.

'Cha,' my dad said. He grabbed our plates and scraped the meatballs on to the copy of the *Daily Mirror*. Then he scraped his own off.

'I'll give them to the dogs,' he said.

We followed him to the front door. He opened it and tossed the meatballs out on to the grey concrete of the yard that the flats were built around. He turned back to us screwing up the paper. 'The dogs can have them. Now eat up the rest or you won't get any peaches.'

The next morning my friend knocked at the door. 'Coming out?' she said.

As I looked at her I could see the meatballs in the yard behind, just where they had landed the night before. No dogs had wanted them either. The light of day made them look like small brown sponges on the ground.

'Have you seen those things?' my friend said, noticing me staring at them. I walked on to the balcony.

'No,' I said innocently. 'What things?'

'Those brown things there,' she said, pointing. 'Nobody knows what they are, they just appeared.'

'Eeehhh – yes,' I said. 'They look horrible. What are they?'

'My mum thinks they're from outa space – she kicked one and it got stuck to her shoe. She had to shake her foot before it would come off.' My friend screwed up her face and I screwed up mine.

'Urghh – they're horrible.' I hoped I was convincing.

I watched people walk through the yard and point at the meatballs and mutter. A dog came and I thought, 'At last they'll be eaten.' But it just sniffed one or two of them and ran away.

'What are they?' I heard two neighbours say as they came along the balcony. 'We'll have to get the caretaker!'

Just as they reached our front door my dad appeared in the doorway. I felt my face flush red.

'Mr Jacobs,' one of the neighbours said, 'have you seen those things in the yard?'

I wanted to block up my ears. I didn't want to hear my dad say, 'What, our old meatballs?' He came out on to the balcony and looked steadily down into the yard. Then he said, 'Oh dear ... what are they?'

'We don't know, they were just there.'

'I think someone must have thrown them out,' the other neighbour added. Everyone nodded in agreement.

'Cha,' my dad said, 'messing up the place like that.' He sucked his teeth and shook his head. 'Some people,' he sighed and smiled.

From *Every Light in the House Burnin'*, published by Headline Book Publishing

From

Gather Together in My Name

Maya Angelou

'Can you cook Creole?'

I looked at the woman and gave her a lie as soft as melting butter. 'Yes, of course. That's all I know how to cook.'

The Creole Café had a cardboard sign in the window which bragged: COOK WANTED. SEVENTY-FIVE DOLLARS A WEEK. As soon as I saw it I knew I could cook Creole, whatever that was.

Desperation to find help must have blinded the proprietress to my age or perhaps it was the fact that I was nearly six feet and had an attitude which belied my seventeen years. She didn't question me about recipes and menus, but her long brown face did trail down in wrinkles, and doubt hung on the edges of her questions.

'Can you start on Monday?'

'I'll be glad to.'

'You know it's six days a week. We're closed on Sunday.'

'That's fine with me. I like to go to church on Sunday.' It's awful to think that the devil gave me that lie, but it came unexpectedly and worked like dollar bills. Suspicion and doubt raced from her face, and she smiled. Her teeth were all the same size, a small white picket fence semi-circled in her mouth.

'Well, I know we're going to get along. You a good Christian. I like that. Yes, ma'am, I sure do.'

My need for a job caught and held the denial.

'What time on Monday?' Bless the Lord!

'You get here at five.'

Five in the morning. Those mean streets before the thugs had gone to sleep, pillowing on someone else's dreams. Before the streetcars began to rattle, their lighted insides like exclusive houses in the fog. Five!

'All right, I'll be here at five, Monday morning.'

'You'll cook the dinners and put them on the steam table. You don't have to do short orders. I do that.'

Mrs Dupree was a short plump woman of about fifty. Her hair was naturally straight and heavy. Probably Cajun Indian, African and white, and naturally, Negro.

'And what's your name?'

'Rita.' Marguerite was too solemn, and Maya too rich-sounding. 'Rita' sounded like dark flashing eyes, hot peppers and Creole evenings with strummed guitars. 'Rita Johnson.'

'That's a right nice name.' Then, like some people do to show their sense of familiarity, she immediately narrowed the name down. 'I'll call you Reet. Okay?'

Okay, of course. I had a job. Seventy-five dollars a week. So I was Reet. Reet, poteet and gone. All Reet. Now all I had to do was learn to cook.

I asked old Papa Ford to teach me how to cook. He had been a grown man when the twentieth century was born, and left a large family of brothers and sisters in Terre Haute, Indiana (always called the East Coast), to find what the world had in store for a 'good-looking coloured boy with no education in his head, but a pile of larceny in his heart'. He travelled with circuses 'shovelling elephant shit'. He then shot dice in freight trains and played koch in back rooms and shanties all over the Northern states.

'I never went down to Hang'em High. Them crackers would have killed me. Pretty as I was, white women was always following me. The white boys never could stand a pretty nigger.'

By 1943, when I first saw him, his good looks were as delicate as an old man's memory, and disappointment rode his face bareback. His hands had gone. Those gambler's fingers had thickened during the Depression, and his only straight job, carpenting, had further toughened his 'moneymakers'. Mother rescued him from a job as a sweeper in a pinochle parlour and brought him home to live with us.

He sorted and counted the linen when the laundry truck picked it up and returned it, then grudgingly handed out fresh sheets to the roomers. He cooked massive and delicious dinners when Mother was busy, and he sat in the tall-ceilinged kitchen drinking coffee by the pots.

Papa Ford loved my mother (as did nearly everyone) with a childlike devotion. He went so far as to control his profanity when she was around, knowing she couldn't abide cursing unless she was the curser.

'Why the sheeit do you want to work in a goddam kitchen?'

'Papa, the job pays seventy-five dollars a week.'

'Busting some goddam suds.' Disgust wrinkled his face.

'Papa, I'll be cooking and not washing dishes.'

'Coloured women been cooking so long, thought you'd be tired of it by now.'

'If you'll just tell me – '

'Got all that education. How come you don't get a goddam job where you can go to work looking like something?'

I tried another tack. 'I probably couldn't learn to cook Creole food, anyway. It's too complicated.'

'Sheeit. Ain't nothing but onions, green peppers and garlic. Put that in everything and you got Creole food. You know how to cook rice, don't you?'

'Yes.' I could cook it till each grain stood separately.

'That's all, then. Them geechees can't live without swamp seed.' He cackled at his joke, then recalled a frown. 'Still don't like you working as a goddam cook. Get married, then you don't have to cook for nobody but your own family. Sheeit.'

The Creole Café steamed with onion vapour, garlic mists tomato fogs and green-pepper sprays. I cooked and sweated among the cloying odours and loved being there. Finally I had the authority I had always longed for. Mrs Dupree chose the daily menu, and left a note on the steam table informing me of her gastronomic decisions. But, I, Rita, the chef, decided how much garlic went into the baked short ribs à la Creole, how many bay leaves would flavour the steamed Shreveport tripe. For over a month I was embroiled in the mysteries of the kitchen with the expectancy of an alchemist about to discover the secret properties of gold.

A leathered old white woman, whom Mother found, took care of my baby while I worked. I had been rather reluctant to leave him in her charge, but Mother reminded me that she tended her white, black and Filipino children equally well. I reasoned that her great age had shoved her beyond the pale of any racial differences. Certainly anyone who lived that long had to spend any unused moments thinking about death and the life to come. She simply couldn't afford the precious time to think of prejudices. The greatest compensation for youth's illness is the utter ignorance of the seriousness of the affliction.

Only after the mystery was worn down to a layer of commonness did I begin to notice the customers. They consisted largely of light-skinned, slick-haired Creoles from Louisiana, who spoke a French patois only a little less complicated than the contents of my pots and equally spicy. I thought it fitting and not at all unusual that they enjoyed my cooking. I was following Papa Ford's instructions loosely and adding artistic touches of my own.

Our customers never ate, paid and left. They sat on the long backless stools and exchanged gossip or shared the patient philosophy of the black South.

'Take it easy, Greasy, you got a long way to slide.'

With the tolerance of ages they gave and accepted advice.

'Take it easy, but take it.'

One large ruddy man, whose name I never knew, allowed his elbows to support him at the twelve-stool counter, and told tales of the San Francisco waterfront: 'They got wharf rats who fight a man flat-footed.'

'No?' A voice wanted to believe.

'Saw one of those suckers the other night backed a cracker up 'gainst a cargo crate. Hadn't been for me and two other guys, coloured guys' – naturally – 'he'd of run down his throat and walked on his liver.'

Near the steam counter, the soft sounds of black talk, the sharp reports of laughter, and the shuffling feet on tiled floors mixed themselves in odorous vapours and I was content.

From *Gather Together in My Name*, published by Virago

Crawfish Love

Ana Castillo

She was my waitress each time I went into Mares Mazatlan but I did not notice her until the third time I was there. They say the third one's the charm or something like that. Anyway, because everyone that worked there wore name tags, I knew her name right away: Catalina. I did not have a name tag — customers obviously are not obliged to wear name tags, and I'm not really accustomed to going around with one on myself, except at regional meetings where we're always required to stick a name tag on, you know? You forget and go around all over town, the gas station attendant and any jerk on the street saying, 'Hello, Vanessa...!' Meanwhile, you keep wondering what the hell's going on — are these guys psychic or something? Then, when you get home your kid brother tells you, 'you can take off the name tag now, stupid'. Then you yourself go, 'Tonta!', and give yourself a slap on the forehead.

Catalina with the name tag and the ruby-red mouth only stared at me kind of funny that day when I said, 'Hey Catalina, what's up?'

She wore her hair real big which was the way younger girls were wearing it at that time – girls in high school, I mean, and girls who were unemployed moms, girls who worked as waitresses. I was a professional so I couldn't go around looking like that anymore. Actually I was in training but at the end of a three-month period, I would be an official sales person at Fuji International Computerware, a huge international company that had just opened up a little branch in our town the year before. I had taken a few computer classes at the tech school while looking for something besides waitressing and cashiering at the local discount stores and I was happy to be alive the day after I put in an application and I got the call that they were interested in checking me out. I felt a little bad for my dad who also went with me to apply, too, because he had been unemployed for a year and there was no hope of him getting his job back since that company had closed down and moved to Mexico.

Mares Mazatlan was a new restaurant, featuring as its specialty crawfish enchiladas. Beaumont is one of the few places, I hear, where you can even get crawfish enchiladas. My girlfriend from Fuji, Eliana, and I, being the only two Mexicans in the training programme, went with our supervisor and two of our co-trainees to check it out. We kind of considered ourselves the experts on Mexican food at Fuji and when we got to Mares Mazatlan we acted like the entire patronage from Fuji depended on our report. Well, this is not at all a story about food so I'll just tell you (just like I've tried to tell Catalina a hundred times but she still doesn't believe me) that although I noticed her the first time I was there I was too wrapped up with trying to impress my colleagues to separate Catalina from her job. And if the truth be known, I only said 'Hi, Catalina, what's up!' to show off in front of them, as if saying hi to the Mexican waitress was something only another Mexican could do. But I liked how waitress-like she conducted herself, filling up our water glasses every five minutes, making sure we did not touch the plates that had obviously been placed on volcanic rock to keep our enchiladas hot. 'No tocan los platos! Están calientes!' she yelled at us; and me and Eliana quickly jumped at the opportunity to translate like we were at the United Nations or something. 'A fine little waitress,' my supervisor from Fuji said when we were dividing up the check. 'Yes, a fine, little waitress, a fine little restaurant,' Eliana echoed and in her way, overdid it just enough, as usual. Eliana was very eager to make a career at Fuji.

I'm ashamed to admit it but on that first official visit, I too thought of Catalina only as a fine little waitress. Actually, she's not that little, and I'm also ashamed to say I didn't notice that either at first. Ambition will do that to you, blind you, leave you like an eyeless crawfish to drag your little, shelly self around without realising what a pathetic creature you are and meanwhile, what? To end the metaphor? We all end up in the same boiling pot in the end.

Nor the second time did I notice Catalina. The second time I actually tried the crawfish enchiladas. Well, I know I said I wouldn't talk about food here but they were pretty good. That's why I decided to go back the following week. This time I did not go with my co-workers who did tend to distract me to no end enough at work, what with all the competition to see which twenty of the forty-two trainees Fuji was going to keep. I was getting worried that, unlike Eliana who worked at perkiness despite her imperfect English, that I just didn't have enough personality to be seen as computer sales finalist material for Fuji.

I went to Mares Mazatlan to drown my sorrows in some crawfish posole, which was their newest specialty.

'What's up, Catalina,' I said, less enthusiastically than when I was with the Fuji crowd. But, as I mentioned earlier, she hardly looked at me anyway, part of the mass blur that made up the luncheon rush, I suppose, and didn't even bother to respond. She came back a minute later and took my order, again, without making eye contact. Without even looking once at me.

Meanwhile between Catalina pouring water into a plastic tumbler she plopped in front of me, wiping the table with a rag and snatching the menu before I finished saying, 'special, plea...', I found myself feeling something that I had not felt before. I shielded my face with my hand, hoping she wouldn't see me blushing. What I was suddenly feeling was something like discovering you're still wearing your name tag on the street, but worse, more like a combination of the name tag, a piece of toilet paper stuck to your shoe when you've come out a public restroom, plus, maybe, discovering afterward that you had a little spinach lodged between your front teeth at that precise moment when you mustered up the courage to say hi to someone you've had a crush on for a month. I said hi again from behind my hand.

I checked my shoes under the table which were okay, noticing Catalina's size sixes while I was looking down there. I can always tell exactly the size a woman wears. I'm giving myself away more than I care to now, but what the hell, which is what I said to Catalina after she let the bowl of crawfish posole hit the table with a pas! so that a few drops of red chile splattered on my only silk blouse. Catalina stared at me but did not apologise.

'Catalina,' I asked, 'you like to play pool?'

From *Loverboys*, published by Norton

This Early

Mei Ng

It is morning and I reach for the brass candlestick by the bed and scrape the wax that dripped down last night. Soon there is a small white pile and for a moment I almost believe it's shredded coconut and want to eat it. I'd be done much quicker if I would just get up and get a knife from the kitchen but I'm not in a hurry. Besides, it doesn't seem right when other people are downstairs chipping away at the icy sidewalk, the frozen steps. All that noise and they've hardly made a dent.

You call to say you're on the way. We hang up quickly as though we can't wait. I brush the wax from my fingers and put the kettle on. Waiting for water to boil is something I don't do. I gather up the garlic skins from the floor, fill the salt shaker, eat a few cashews. There is hardly anything in the refrigerator a couple of old yams, some lemons, a green pepper that's only starting to cave in on itself. It makes you nervous that I keep so little food in the house.

You walk quickly to my apartment, our morning bagels tucked inside your jacket, close to your body. When you get here, they are still warm so that the butter melts. We both hate margarine. You say, 'What if there's a big storm and I can't make it over here, what will you eat?' You've known me a week, but already you know how I hate going out in the mornings.

I try to explain that it only looks like I have no food. In an emergency, I could whip something up. When there's too much food in the fridge I get edgy, afraid I won't get around to it. It's like I'm always waiting for food to go bad, so I can throw it out already.

I wait for the water to really get going before I make the tea. I make your cup first, you like strong tea. I let it steep, then add lots of lemon, lots of honey. Then I make my tea with your old tea bag. I take my tea light, like old ladies at the diner. If it's too strong, I can't sleep at night.

You show me pictures from your trip to China. For a white girl, you look pretty good in your red imperial robe and headpiece, standing by the palace. You hold your neck very still so the headpiece doesn't tilt you over. It's heavier than it looks. You tell me you are angry at your mother for not teaching you Italian, that all you have left is lots of ways to cook pasta and a big family. I tell you my second language is Spanish, not Chinese. As I look at the photo of you by the Great Wall, I remember that your boyfriend is Asian, too, and I wonder if you've got some fetish thing going on. But then you are talking and touching my arm at the same time, and I think: Everyone's going to China these days, it doesn't mean anything. Me? No, I've never been.

The phone rings. The machine clicks on and then there's my father's voice in my room. 'Hello, Daisy? Did you go out yet? It's slippery out there. I almost fell down when I go out to shovel. You be careful when you go down your stair,' he says. Then he's quiet but doesn't hang up right away like there's something else he wants to say but can't remember what it is. He clears his throat, then it sounds like he's trying to hang up but can't quite fit the phone back together again.

'Was that your father? He sounds sweet,' you say.

'My father? Sweet? I guess so,' I say because there isn't enough time to explain him. It would take all day, all night even, and you like to get back early.

My bagel is too big and doughy, each bit seems a lot of work. You don't eat your bagel either. We cover our plates with napkins and tell each other how we normally eat, tons and tons. We're just not hungry right now. Maybe later.

We say something about the weather, about how important the right boots are. You are not looking at me, you are talking and looking down at the floor. The more you touch my arm, the faster you talk. Your mouth is moving and I am looking at it.

Later that afternoon, we are on the couch, its velvet worn almost smooth as your skin. You tell me you've never done anything like this before. Outside, it sounds like everyone on the block is chopping ice. There is still so much to break up and push away.

My wrist is thin next to yours. Your arms just a little bigger than mine. I ask you if you work out and you say only at your job, emptying bags of ice into the bin, reaching for bottles on the upper shelf. You say you hate all the people who come to drink in the afternoon but when they don't come, you miss them.

I ask about the scar on your arm, near the curve of your elbow. It's so light you can hardly see it anymore. I put my lips to it as you tell me, 'I used to clean my grandmother's chandelier. Her eyes were huge behind her glasses but still, she couldn't see so good. Her hand was always moving on the table, reaching for things she couldn't see. One day when I was cleaning, I moved too close to one of the bulbs. I'm always burning myself.' I show you my hands, all the little scars. I don't have to worry about burns, but keep me away from glass.

You say you want a picture of me to take with you. I bring out my shoebox and you pick the one of me in my orange sun hat, running on the beach. It's hard to tell what direction I'm running in.

You put the picture in your bag, then pile on all the layers again – you are well prepared for winter. I hate socks and hats, I can stay in for days. I wonder if I'm getting like my father. He doesn't like to go out of the house, doesn't like putting on shoes, says they hurt his feet. He still dresses every day in a white shirt and neatly pressed pants, but on his feet are those old gladiator slippers.

'What are you doing for the rest of the night?' you ask me.

'Oh, I don't know,' I say. 'This and that.'

'Are you going to read, cook dinner, go out?' you say. You are completely dressed and it's hot in my apartment. I see that you don't want to think of me just sitting here in the same position all night.

'Yeah, I think I'll read, make a little dinner,' I say, so you can leave. I listen to your boots going down the stairs, then out the door. There is no sound as you make your way down the icy stairs. I listen for the gate opening and closing, then I start chipping away at the wax again. I am working faster now, digging with my nails. There is more ice out there than anyone is used to.

I saw someone fall yesterday. She got to the corner and slid off the curb. Her legs folded under her and she crumpled gently as though she were tired of walking and just wanted a little rest before going on.

I call home. I want to ask my mother how to make her sea bass with black bean sauce. Not that I have the ingredients, but just listening to how she makes it would be enough. My mother always gave me the best bits. After she drizzled the sesame oil over the top, she'd remove the backbone with her chopsticks. She would check to see if there were any little bones left, then she'd put a good piece in my bowl.

My father answers the phone. He says, 'Your mother?' like he doesn't know who I'm talking about. 'She went shopping. Again. It's been four hours since she left the house. She took the cart with her. The refrigerator is so full you can't fit anything else in it. There's food all over the house. She buy, buy, buy, then she forget about it. How much can two old people eat?'

The next morning when you come over, it is the same with the bagels. We butter them but don't eat them. Today we don't talk about the weather. Today you're the one to say, 'Let's sit on the couch where it's more comfortable.' We start ever so slowly.

'I don't know what to do. Help me – you've done this before, yes?' you say.

Have I touched you before – here, and here? No, but I've wanted to for a long time. I don't say this to you.

'Yes? With other women?' you say.

'A little, just a little. A long time ago,' I say. I don't want you to think I know what I'm doing either.

Afterwards, we are finally hungry. You have dinner plans in a couple of hours, but you want to eat now. Even though it's only afternoon, I cook those two steaks that I had in the freezer. Sweet potato fries and a salad. See, didn't I tell you I had food?

I watch you cutting into your steak and you're not the least bit squeamish. You take yours medium rare. All that blood. You tell me you don't want to hurt your boyfriend's feelings. He is a nice man, you tell me, easy to be with. He shaves before coming to bed so as not to bristle you. You don't know whether to tell him or not. I wonder whether you will eat two dinners.

It is time for you to leave, but we both want another cup of tea. I rinse the cups from breakfast and make your tea first. You drink it so dark. How can you sleep at night? You tell me to use a new bag for myself, but isn't it just a waste if I take it light anyway?

At my mother's house, she makes tea in the old blue-and-white pot that she's had forever. If you want it light, you take the first cup. If you want it darker, you have to wait a little longer. I used to have a teapot. It was ivory-coloured, squat and small. First the knob on the lid fell off. Then the spout got chipped and finally the handle. I saved the pieces for a while, meaning to glue them back together.

Downstairs, there are kids going door to door, with shovels over their shoulders. 'Shovel your walk, mister? Just three dollars for the whole sidewalk. The steps, too.' People have taken to using axes and hammers like they are angry.

It is dark and I light a candle. Just one. The wax doesn't start falling right away. It collects at the top, then pours down all at once. Tomorrow there will be white dots stuck to the floor.

When you tell him about me, he doesn't seem to mind too much. 'It's just kissing, isn't it?' he says. With him it's easy, you tell me, he's the boy and you're the girl. You've had lots of practice and you're good at it. When I come to see you at your job, tending bar, I see how much money the men leave on the counter.

It would be mean to leave your boyfriend when he hasn't done anything wrong. He's sweet, you tell me, a nice man. It's not that I think you're lying. I've known lots of nice men; I was married to one. Daniel would cook brown rice for me even though he hated the smell, said it smelled like mouse droppings. But he could never get it quite right. I would tell him to use more water, cook it over a slow flame. But somehow, it was always too hard. I had to put it back in the pot, add more water and cook it some more. But I would kiss him when I did this so he wouldn't feel bad.

You don't tell your boyfriend what you tell me, that when we're together, you don't have to be the girl, the woman; you don't have to be all the women on billboards smiling with their mouths open, their eyes closed. You don't have to hold in your stomach. You can just be a plain old person. This is scary to you, you're not sure how to do this.

One afternoon you say you will brush my hair for me. You brush slowly, starting at the bottom and working your way up. I can tell from the way you hold the brush that you've had long hair before. Now your hair is cut close to your head. As you pull the brush down my back, I remember that Daniel would brush my hair. After a while he could do it like you are doing now, but in the beginning he'd try to undo the knots in one stroke and ended up pulling my hair out. As you brush, slow and steady, I start to cry. You do not stop.

I had a friend once in the sixth grade. Her name was Marianne Shirts and there was no television in her house. I would sleep over, wearing one of her nightgowns that seemed softer than mine and I would brush her hair a hundred times before we went to bed. After we got under the covers we would practise kissing. At first her tongue was a surprise, something I wouldn't have thought of myself. Then after a while, our nightgowns would ride up to our waists and our bare legs touching was another surprise. I was afraid that I would like practising too much, that I would like it better than the real thing. One night when Marianne turned to me and said 'Wanna practise', I made myself say no thanks, like she had offered me a hot chocolate or a peanut butter cookie. I stayed up all night watching her eyes move back and forth under her lids.

After you leave, my mother calls me. First, pick a sea bass with clear eyes, not cloudy. When you get home, wash it in cold water, inside and out. Make sure there aren't any scales left on it. Soak the black beans in some warm water. Put the fish in a bowl, chop garlic, scallion, and ginger. Pour a little soy sauce on it, not too much. Then, steam it until it's done, maybe twenty minutes. Heat some peanut oil in a pan until it's very hot, but not smoky, add a few drops of sesame, pour it on top. Watch out for small bones.

Sometimes in the evenings, you go into your kitchen to call me. I hold the phone close to my ear; you are talking softly. I wonder what your kitchen looks like and I imagine you leaning your head against wallpaper that was pretty when it was new but is faded now and buckled in spots. I'm sure that in reality the walls are painted a pale yellow and I try to imagine that, but I'm too busy wondering what your boyfriend is doing while you're whispering in the kitchen.

'I know I can't ask you to wait for me,' you say.

'But wait for you?' I say.

You have known your boyfriend for three years but now he feels alien to you. You say that sometimes when you are in bed with him, you close your eyes and pretend it's me. This is not much consolation. When you tell him you want to keep seeing me, he says 'Sure, why not?' but then he gets real quiet. You ask him what he's thinking and he says, 'Should we catch a movie tonight, or just stay in?' Later when he fucks you, he does it rough and you like it at first. Afterwards, he says, 'You shouldn't lead that woman on like that.'

I would like to ask you why you keep my picture in your lingerie drawer. You tell me it makes you happy whenever you go to put on your bra and there's my face. The picture of you is by my bed. Next to the one of my mother. The one where she's sixteen and her face is smooth and white as the inside of a bowl. Her face isn't really white, that's just powder. It's the picture that made my father go all the way across the ocean in a boat called *The Wilson*, of all things.

'Ma, did you love him then?'

'Nah, I thought he was mean, he looked like a gangster.'

'Did you grow to love him, Ma?'

'Love? Chinese people don't believe in love.'

It is night and all the shutters are closed. I think of you and even my teeth ache with wanting. I wait for the sound of chopping to stop, but there is so much ice. It's stupid to start waiting for spring this early.

From *Tasting Life Twice*, edited by E J Levy, published by Avon Books

My Mistake

Stevie Davies

'I'll put on my chef's hat and cook you up a little something.'

'Oh, no, really, don't go to any bother.'

'None in the world. Can't wait to see you.'

For a struggling young artist like myself, the Leeds exhibition, an invitation to lecture, and the attention of the eminent art historian who was to be my host were unlooked-for opportunities which made my heart beat high with excitement. I'd familiarised myself with his newest book on still life, *Fruits of Earth and Art*.

Gerald would meet me on the platform. Just let him know the time to the nearest minute: he liked to be punctual. His voice on the phone was affable, elderly. I pictured him as rotund, carpet slippered.

'My wife – sadly passed away – would have adored to

meet you. Now *she* was a cook if you like. And painted a little too.'

These wistful words stuck in my mind. I thought of him grieving through long autumn evenings. But he'd assured me he kept cheerful, seldom allowing himself to brood. Perhaps, I thought, as the train drew in, my presence would take his mind off his loss; in turn I might confide in him.

Alighting, I realised my mistake.

My mistake strode towards me, arms wide. My mistake embraced me like a lover, implanting kisses on both cheeks. I staggered backwards into the spike of a traveller's umbrella.

'Can't be as bad as that! Can it?'

'Pardon?'

'The shock of seeing me at last – *in the flesh.*'

I could not (staring up into the ageing boyishness of his face) rid my mind of the word 'flesh'. And 'flesh' begat 'fish': a cold fish, I thought, as his hand sidled familiarly between my arm and my chest. I flinched away.

'It's super to see you. Come along.' He swooped on my case and portfolio: I followed my possessions out of the station.

'A teensy bit of drizzle,' said my host. 'Hence the hat.'

From beneath the tweed hat-brim, two milky-blue eyes peeped with simpering but lofty benignity.

'I always carry my own case.'

'Certainly not. You're *my guest.*'

The word 'guest' was posted in to join its companions, 'fish' and 'in the flesh'. I itched at being a guest in the flesh but counselled myself to be sensible. There was no harm in him, I reasoned – he's just affectionate and maybe nervous. I am habitually shy.

We tracked down Gerald's car amongst copious puddles. He knew he'd parked it somewhere in the general vicinity and he knew it was red.

'*Here* she is! Naughty girl, where did you get to? She needs spanking, doesn't she?' Then, raising the boot, he winked, adding, 'Or someone else does!'

Who did he mean? Him or me? I stared, glazed.

'Only one of my jokes,' he explained, and gambolled round the car. 'You'll get used to them. In you get, poor wet girl. Can't wait to feed and nurture you.'

I hastily locked my seat-belt, to pre-empt offers of help. Gerald sketched the evening's programme: first (since he had failed – naughty him – to buy in provisions) shopping for comestibles in a superior area of Leeds; home; snack and settle in; out for my lecture at the Art Gallery when he'd drink in my delicious wisdom; back for supper (did I like aubergines?) and, at whatever time I decreed, Bed.

Bed. It was spoken with a capital letter.

I mentioned my partner, Jo.

Gerald seemed not to hear.

I perused the rainy windows, wondering how his wife died.

'The greengrocer we're going to meet,' said Gerald, leading me through the rainswept streets, '... is most unusual. I hope you'll like him (there's no doubt he'll go overboard for you), he's no ordinary shopkeeping type ... his interests (which I have sought to foster) go far beyond cauliflowers – they include not only Rotary but – ' he roared against the wind, 'ART!'

'Oh. Is it far? I don't want to be late for my lecture and I need to ... you know ... compose myself beforehand.'

'No, no. Just over there, round the corner. Is her strength failing?' He bent solicitously. Lest he berate himself as a naughty boy, I shook my head, and we pressed on through the downpour.

Loitering by the potatoes, I feigned to assess them, while my mistake hail-fellowed the greengrocer standing by his till, brawny arms folded. Though Gerald, wafting and swaying over him, was the taller man, the greengrocer was easily the stronger. If he undertook to punch my companion on the nose, as he had motive and apparent inclination to do, it would be a knock-out blow.

' ... so, you elected to take the coach-trip to see the Magrittes after all ... I reverence Magritte ... so you went by *coach*?'

He paused.

The greengrocer said, 'Aye.'

'Did they exceed expectations?' Gerald waited rapt, yellow plastic shopping bag dangling, hands clasped.

'Aye.'

'*Wonderful*,' gushed Gerald. 'I *knew* they'd ravish your soul. And your wife's of course. Did she accompany you?'

'Aye.'

'Dear me, I was forgetting our errand, in the glow of our delightful conversation.'

The greengrocer's fibres seemed to relax. I straightened up from my tense crouch by the potatoes.

'I've a treat for you both.' Extending his arms, Gerald impelled us together. 'I must introduce my young friend, a well-known Artist, Ms Zoë Jones (note – Ms), she is exhibiting at the Whalley. This, Zoë dear, is Mr Freddy Waters, an Art-Lover.'

'And what do you paint?' spat out the greengrocer.

'Oh – I'm ... not well known,' I muttered, as a shopper shoved her basket of apples past me on to the counter. 'But I like vegetables. And ... I feel perhaps we ought to buy some, Gerald, and stop blocking the queue.'

The greengrocer's smile was warm with fellow-feeling.

'Such an amiable fellow,' said Gerald by the sweet peppers. 'Too discerning a mind really for all these veggies. Still, one must eat. And what shall we eat, my dear? You choose.' His expressive arm waved to include all nature's bounty, arrayed shelf beyond shelf.

'I've no idea. I'm worried about my lecture – getting there on time ...'.

'We've oodles of time. Let us select only the most sensual vegetables ... Now you look puzzled. And looking puzzled becomes you. But there is more. You look ... am I right? ... Shocked? ... You're quivering. Aren't you?'

'No.'

'Quite right. You shouldn't. After all, an Artist perceives the sensual qualities of fruits and vegetables – the palate and the palette – consider this lemon, for instance, as the object of a still life.'

He thrust the lemon beneath my nose.

'Sniff.'

I sniffed.

He tossed the lemon into the air. I caught the green-grocer's eye.

'It isn't still life, is it, if you're throwing it around? I think we should put it down or buy it, and I should prepare for my lecture.'

'Little *bourgeoise*. She's degenerating into a consumer,' Gerald reproved. 'The cultivated eye should savour the colours, shape, texture of ... for instance, aubergines. What's your view of aubergines?'

Smilingly he inclined his head, in sign that I was to deliver some ingenious or tender observation concerning this vegetable.

'I've never tried one.'

'Never – tried – one! This poor girl,' Gerald advised the shop, 'has never tasted aubergines. Let me introduce her to the Fair Unknown.'

He cradled one, fingering the soft give of purple flesh. Delicate fingertips conveyed the produce to his puckered mouth, which imprinted a kiss, gazing into my eyes. He winked, I winced.

'Now you.'

'Oh no.' Hot-faced, I turned to the mushrooms. 'I like mushrooms,' I admitted in panic. 'And carrots.'

'You shall have them *all*,' he promised, shovelling vegetables into brown paper bags. 'I'll flash-fry them in my wok, specially for you. Do you possess a wok?' he asked the greengrocer.

'Nope.'

'Ah but you *must* get one, without delay.' While Gerald praised woks, our purchases were rung up. It seemed life could not properly continue without a wok. Gerald's Chinese woman-friend had taught him wok arts.

'Don't expect perfection though. I never cooked until poor Nora died. Nora wouldn't let me in the kitchen.'

Perhaps the kitchen, I reflected, was Nora's only refuge. But then, glimpsing an inscrutable grimace, I chided myself for lack of charity. Probably Gerald had only become peculiar after his bereavement. Reluctant pity spasmed in my heart.

'You must be lonely,' I volunteered as we exited. The greengrocer seemed to buckle at the knees and a snort or guffaw followed us into the street.

'*Very*. But sweet friends mitigate my solitude – my young Chinese friend; my lodger a German Assistantin; my four Slovakian lady visitors; my angelic daughters; Dr Sara Weinberg from Boston – and now there's *you*! My cup runneth over.'

He charged me merrily into a delicatessen where a man up a ladder was greeted as a bosom friend and introduced to Zoë the Famous Artist.

'Hi.' The man up the ladder with a frozen smile refrained from coming down.

'Hi.'

'I've been describing your *wonderful* shop to my young friend,' enthused my companion. 'And we're going to buy something,' he promised, as a rare treat for the man up the ladder. 'But ... where's that flipping list?' He emptied out the vegetables in his search. 'Extend your mind in this super place, Zoë, by pondering the exotic wonders of the salami and those olives ... over there, see ... and he paused, suspending his rummaging. 'Now, of what do they remind you?'

Impossible to maintain my attitude of compassion when similitudes between olives and the eyes of dusky Italian signorinas were struck.

Bottled addled eyes stared unblinkingly into mine.

We purchased three croissants.

Out on the pavement it was snowing. 'Not tired, are you? Goodie, because we can't manage without pud for tonight.'

'I don't ... need ... a pudding. Thank you. I'd rather rest before my lecture.'

'Nonsense! You're just saying that to be polite. It's *no trouble whatsoever.*'

Laden with three types of pud; one bunch of grapes (seedless) which my host vowed to pop individually in my mouth in his ceaseless quest for my wellbeing; but no choccies because of his regard for my sylph-like figure (certain to be sylph-like though so far teasingly incognito beneath that capacious coat), we returned to the car.

'At home, you'll put your feet up and let me serve you. What would you like, some lovely hot soup?'

'I'd love a cup of tea.'

'Soup is so nourishing – so warming to the cockles. What are cockles by the way? "Cockles of your heart" – curious phrase. Does your heart have cockles, Zoë?'

'I don't know but all I need is a cup of tea before my lecture. If it's no trouble.'

'But I *want* to take trouble. For *you.*' He steered with one hand, his free hand for an instant visiting my knee. I shrank; swivelled. The hand, gliding to the gear lever, seemed to deposit a chilly spoor. My pent irritation erupted.

'I don't want a cup of nourishing soup! I want a cup of tea!'

'Onion or asparagus?'

I stared and shouted again.

'*Tea*, please, *not – soup.*'

'Good, because we're right out of tea. I don't drink it myself though Gisela may have some camomile in the cupboard. You don't drink much tea?'

'*Yes*. I *love* tea. I drink it all the time. PG Tips.'

'No, I'm not keen either. Prefer soup any day. Or gin. Do you go for gin? Nora hated gin. Hid the bottle in the airing cupboard. One of her endearing little oddities, bless her darlingness.'

Nora glared from the mantelpiece. Wherever you stood, Nora's eyes avoided your solicitation. Grey hair helmeted a tense face above a body huddled from the camera's mortifying stare. She grasped a kitchen-knife. The cameraman appeared to have stolen upon her privacy whilst slicing up a cucumber, a violation she swore to avenge.

'Ah,' exclaimed my mistake, 'you've met Nora.' He sighed. 'Never happier. Nora was never happier than when preparing a picnic. This was in California. A happy, happy time. Never again – nevermore ... She was a leetle bit cross actually, about being snapped. Camera-shy. We only have two other photos of her. Keep meaning to frame this one.' He gazed with dolorous fondness at the wilted picture.

'If you don't, I suppose it will fade.'

'All beautiful things fade,' murmured Gerald. 'And perish.'

'If you frame it,' (I rephrased more optimistically, to

disperse his melancholy), 'it *won't* fade.'

'How very sweet you are,' he looked up. 'My kind Zoë. I'm a poor playfellow, dear Zoë (what a smashing name that is — Zoë, Zoë, buzzing like a little bee — stingless, of course, in your case). — A forlorn widower is no companion for a lovely young woman. Do remove that coat, dear; let me see you as you truly are.'

I hugged the coat around me with a shiver. We'd be going out again soon. And it was so snowy.

Chuckling, he swept out; breezed back in, bearing a loaded tray.

'Pot of tea for one — jug of milk — assorted biscuits. I was just teasing you about the soup. Afraid you'll find me a tease. But you don't mind, do you, Zoë, an old man's harmless pranks?'

Evidently Gerald's harmless pranks had fatigued him more than either of us had been aware. For during my lecture he dozed, sprawled in his anorak, jerking when beset by dreams. The nine persons comprising the remainder of the audience seemed scarcely more conscious, as I talked them through my work. One, muttering about the wrong lecture, crashed out. The remnant sat somnolent, in the dim, echoing vault. Meaty-thighed nudes by a rival artist bestrode the walls, against which my words faltered, boomed and died. An hour later the sleepers awoke, wine being announced. Gerald stretched his limbs, smiling like a pink baby fresh from his bath; at the pop of a wine-cork he cantered to the table where he secured a whole bottle — *'Pour Mademoiselle la Jeune Artiste!'* — which he liberally sampled.

'I'm purring,' he assured me. 'Purring like a stroked tomcat basking before a coal fire — that's the effect your talk has had on me. Aren't you purring?' he enquired of an elderly woman who had summoned courage to come up to speak to me.

As she and I conversed, Gerald's face tilted from one to the other between swigs, smiling away as if crooning some saucy private tune.

'Nice talking to you, dear,' said the woman to me warmly.

'Nice talking to you too.'

'Little old ladies,' pronounced my host, swaying still to the unheard melody, 'come to these do's ... don't understand a word of what's said.'

I pondered bolting into the night. But my case with my money and chequebook was locked in Gerald's house.

'I'm a little-old-lady-to-be and please don't call me darling. Do you mind if we go now Gerald: I want to ...'

'Of course, angel being.' Waving to the few remaining guzzlers, he whirled me off to the car.

The German Assistantin, a tall, blond, red-nosed girl in her mid-twenties, exchanged three affectionate continental kisses with her landlord. She appeared entirely normal, even down to the head-cold which she termed a dratted thing.

I congratulated her on her impeccable English.

'Oh, thank Gerald for that. He brings me on most incorrigibly.'

We all three laughed.

'Gisela *süsses Kind*, we don't say "incorrigibly" in this context,' he said, pouring sherry, 'unless we wish to be terribly wicked.'

'My mistake. I labour *frightfully* hard Zoë and still I find English a most puzzling tongue.'

Gisela confounded me. If such a nice girl felt safe lodging with Gerald, I reasoned, draining my glass, surely he must be a harmless enough chap, perhaps a little 'inadequate' (an oddly soothing word). A post-lecture sherry-glow suffused my mind.

'Well, must toddle,' said Gerald. 'Must feed my honoured guest. Feet up on this pouffe, I insist, Zoë. No, I insist! Will you eat with us, Gisela darling? There's plenty of *gnocchi* for three ... Oh, *do*. Don't disappoint me.'

My sense of safety again increased at Gerald's willingness to be chaperoned.

'I must my dratted cold nurse,' said Gisela, declining, and sneezed profusely. 'Gerald is most sweet to me. He rent me my room for a peanut. And he tolerates my boyfriend. I have only praise for his good virtues.'

I was browsing through Gerald's celebrated book on Barbara Hepworth when my aproned host trundled in a trolley.

'To us!' Clinking glasses, we essayed the *gnocchi*. From high walls, oil-painted faces of minor Leeds dignitaries appraised my progress through oily vegetables straight from the wok.

'Now that our hunger is sated a *soupçon*, you must tell me about yourself. *May* I ask something?'

'Of course,' I faltered.

'Forgive me if it seems a cheek ... but during your "green" abstract period, what was the function of the *pointilliste* carmine dots on the top swathe of the pictures?'

Flattered at being attributed with artistic 'periods' at the age of twenty-eight and with having my red blodges dignified under the denomination *pointillisme*, I discoursed freely on my work, Gerald astutely commenting, comparing me rather favourably with the youthful Matisse. Wine flowed.

'How blessed I am,' breathed Gerald, and sat back, surrendering his napkin, as if spiritually replete, 'to have the company at my simple supper of a distinguished artist.'

'Well, hardly distinguished ...'

'... which modesty on your part emboldens me to ask a scarcely less familiar question.'

'Ask away.'

'Why do you eschew male models?'

'Er ... I just prefer females.'

'*Ah* ... thought so. Have some pud.'

'Just a few grapes perhaps.'

'But we have three kinds of pud, Zoë. It would be outrageous not to do justice to the Gateway luxury trifle ... Of course you've room, don't be a silly girl, I'll smack your fingers.'

A spoonful of trifle flopped into my bowl.

'Afterwards I'll pop those grapes one by one into your little moist rosebud mouth. As I promised.'

Pangs of dismay stirred; yet I sat immobile, like one in a trance. Why couldn't I move? Why? *Just get out of here,* a voice advised.

'Actually I'm awfully tired,' I said. 'I think I'll ...' Rejecting a phrase containing the word 'bed' as excessively suggestive, I fell back on 'retire'. I would run up, grab my case, and escape.

'As I *promised,*' Gerald repeated, as though he hadn't heard. 'Pop 'em in one by one. So sensuous. So innocent. I never break my promises. It's my rule. And then I'll ...'

'Gerald, I don't want grapes, I insist on ...' I stood up, face burning, and my chair fell back. It was not fear I experienced but frantic social embarrassment.

'... model for you.'

'*What?*'

'Ah, little Zoë, I'm guessing now but my guess is you don't know the full-blooded thrill of being with a Real Man. If I can pinpoint any weakness in your Art, here it is, don't you see? Don't contradict. Such delicate sensibility ... so vulnerable and, oh, infinitely tender, when one has won her trust. But has one won?'

As my mistake advanced round the table, I retreated. And still it was not terror that muted me but an agony of social mortification rendering me awkward as a callow girl of sixteen.

'Oh!' I squealed.

His sock was off; his tie.

His trousers fell, and his pants came down.

His shirt was peeled over his head, followed by a string vest.

'Here I am,' Gerald informed me.

And he twirled on the spot to manifest his all. Over the winking crystal and cutlery, the wreckage of the oleaginous vegetables and fresh fruit salad with mangos, a nude man in late middle age exhibited his bony charms. His genital organ dangled flaccid. 'What do you think?' he enquired.

'Not much.' I strove for nonchalance. 'You'll get cold.'

'Just what Nora would have said! You'd have got on, you two: pity you never had the chance to meet.'

'Put your clothes back on please and let me out. Or I'll scream.'

'Dear one ... Zoë ... you're not ... but, yes, you are, you are ... shocked ... *aren't* you?' He seemed genuinely amazed. His hands fell limp at his shanks. 'I thought ... as an artist ... you'd be more liberated. Oh my poor girl, I've shocked you. Now I can't forgive myself – I really can't. Half a mo, I'll don my apron. There, that's better, you're not shocked *now*, are you?' asked the solicitous nude in the floral apron.

'Could I just get my case and leave? I'd really rather ... I insist on going home.'

'Sweetest, have I scared you?' His jacket was now on, and one sock. He was pulling up his pants as a matter of urgency. 'Look, just let me make it up to you. I've been a daft boy. It's past midnight – you can't get home now. Look here, we'll give those grapes a miss.'

The apron was off, his trousers zipped up.

'Do you do this kind of thing to Gisela?' Curiosity overcame me. 'Or your four Slovakian ladies? Is this treat offered to all your female visitors? – or am I specially favoured?'

'Of course you've a right to ask that question,' he acknowledged, but seemed hurt at my crude failure to comprehend the hospitable intent informing all his actions. He piled crockery on the trolley, tying on the apron again. 'Yes, I understand *why* you feel compelled to ask it,' he reiterated in a choked voice. 'But Zoë, be assured, you've entirely mistaken my drift. Don't worry, I'm not upset.'

'Oh dear.' I followed him and the trolley through to the kitchen. In need of some refreshing draught, he took a deep sniff of some carnations in a vase, before method- ically stacking the pots on the counter-top.

'I'll not wash up tonight,' he informed me. 'But I hate leaving mess down here. Don't offer to help, I forbid it, you're my guest. Now what else is there to do before bed? Locked up, haven't I? Yes. Can't be too careful, with all these burglaries. I've installed a jolly expensive electronic system which means no one can get *in* or *out*. A beetle would be detected. No joke. Now then ... light off in here. Go through, I'm right behind you ... Now it's time for beddybyes. Gisela's in the attic, by the way, in the land of nod. Wonderful, the way they built these spacious Victorian houses, no need for sound-proofing, I never even hear her TV. But before we enter the arms of Morpheus, Zoë, just tell the penitent he's forgiven.'

He extended a hand, in the echoing stairwell. I hesitated.

'Won't you trust me?'

'Yes, of course.' It was a verbal reflex, bred of a childhood schooled in good manners. But my hand stayed bunched in my pocket.

'Ah,' he sighed. '*Now* I'm happy. *Now* you've made me happy, Zoë. Just give your hand as a friend – as artist to art historian – and grant me the benison of your trust.'

'Can I make a phone call?'

'My pleasure. Phone's in my bedroom.'

'Well, perhaps I won't bother. Goodnight then.' I attempted to sidle past.

But he wrapped me in his arms.

I struggled and squirmed. 'Got you, you little tease,' he laughed into my hair.

'I'm – not – teasing. Get – off – me.'

'But I want you to say you trust me. And I want to tell you there are' (he whispered) 'bananas and fresh warm croissants for breakfast ... And would you like me to come into bed and cuddle you?' he asked fondly, as a final charity he could dispense.

'No. *No.*'

'Well, it's not compulsory.'

'No – because if it were, it would be rape.'

The word *rape* resounded in the stairwell. I dashed up the stairs, past the twin dead partridges lying tastefully on a silver platter beside a gun; past Mr Wedgwood Pritchard of Oakwood Lodge mounted on a bay mare and fingering his whip; past a surprising ironing board almost blocking my door, which collapsed with a crash as I thrust it aside.

'What a thing to say,' I heard my pained host reflect. 'She *must* be tired, poor dear.'

Shooting the lock, I plugged the keyhole with paper; sat; shook; waited. Up the stairs footsteps advanced. Halfway up they paused. Brandishing in both hands a cricket bat from a display of childhood memorabilia on a shelf, I positioned myself behind the door. If he came for me I would whack him where it hurt. I would. I'd whack him.

Yet I felt more foolish than terrified or purposeful. Embarrassed at my inability to control or abort the situation, I was ashamed, precisely, of my shame.

He wound the antique clock on the bend in the stair. Immediately, it chimed, with a silvery cadence.

'Ah, lovely! lovely!' exclaimed its owner, in a little fit of beatitude. And on he climbed, footsteps tapping on polished boards until they paused on my landing. I heard the swish of long velvet curtains being pulled.

'Nighty night my gentle Desdemona,' came his voice.

I fiercely swung back my cricket bat. My heart pounded.

'My door's ajar, should you want me in the night.'

The footsteps receded; the toilet flushed; the lights went out. Laying the bat on my white counterpane, I considered strategy. Insofar as I was locked into this room, I was safe. Insofar as I was locked into this fortress of a house, I was imprisoned. Insofar as I needed excruciatingly to relieve myself, I was on the horns of a dilemma.

Hours later I crept out fully-dressed but barefoot, bat in hand, my sensitive bladder swollen and hurting. Holding my breath, I tiptoed past his door; locked myself in; galloped back to my sanctuary. The bat shared my bed that night and the clock-chime kept us informed of the passing quarters.

Morning dawned. Up he got, irrepressibly cheerful, to waltz past my door and shoot apart the velvet curtains; and he was carolling – some nursery rhyme – what was he singing? – 'Girls and boys come out to play – '. Then off down the stairs. Clicking heels chased busily to and fro.

'Coo-ee! Zo-ee!' called Gerald up the stairs. 'Brekkie when you're ready!'

Freedom was within my sights. Clutching case and portfolio, I peered over the banister, uncertain how to proceed, desperate to avoid that bland simper, above which the pale eyes did not smile at all. Again I rued my impotence: instead of storming down powered by righteous ire, I was cringing with stage fright in the wings of some *farceur*'s play. Last night's charade had been avoidable. If I had asserted myself ... summoned the *savoir faire* to laugh him down ... but I hadn't. Now I crouched in coat and scarf, loitering at the head of the stairs wondering if the front door was still locked while ... a fool with a banana in one hand and a croissant in the other frolicked into the hallway, waving first one and then the other at me.

'I can't decide,' he called up, 'which my Zoë prefers ... the long yellow one or the deliciously crumbly flaky melt-in-the-mouth croissant. Enlighten me .... Whatever's the matter, little tragic girl?' he asked, at the sight of my exhausted, aghast face; and began to mount towards me.

I flinched back. The doorbell rang. Down he leapt and flung it open.

'Ivy! It's you!' he chirruped to his cleaning woman, as if his heart's desire had materialised.

While he fussed her over the threshold, I grasped my opportunity – charged downstairs – past the pair of them – out of the gate – down the hill, into a misty autumnal morning, not looking back lest I encounter that tall spectre striding after me in tender remonstrance.

Three days later, my cold having fully developed, a letter arrived.

'My darlingest Zoë,' it began, 'Despite non-arrival of your bread-and-butter letter (*do use a first class stamp*) I cannot deny myself the exquisite gratification of penning you a line. For in writing, I fancy I see your form and face in the room, shooting me that douce, raffish, quizzical look – which has changed the world for me. Gentlest Zoë, with your tentative, afraidy looks. You were so good to me. Bliss that I could make you feel at home – ply you with licorice comforts. Sweet Gisela should have cooked my birthday meal tonight, but her cold is so rotten she feels she must stay in bed so I am a tidgy bit bereft – but widowers must be stoical and endure etcetera. I can lie in your place in the bed you honoured with the grace of your person. It used to be mine, you know, so in a sense you were not alone in it ...'

'No, I damned well wasn't,' I said to Jo. 'I had the cricket bat in there with me.'

'Shall I phone the creep?' asked Jo.

'No, don't bother. He's harmless. At least I think he is.'

From The Fires of Bride

Ellen Galford

Aaaahhhh ...' says Catriona, swirling her glass and inhaling the vapours. 'A year of sunshine and splendour. The world breathing a sigh of relief. The first decent vintage after the war. You can almost see that far away summer when you taste it. Go on ... no, don't guzzle it, girl! Sip ... just a little bit ... draw it through your teeth, swirl it around, think about it, listen to what it tells you, then swallow it. That's right. Pure nectar ...'

Maria has successfully negotiated the lobster soup, but the main course is proving more of a challenge.

'Now tell me about yourself,' commands Catriona, staring hawklike at Maria as she deftly carves the slices of roast island lamb, pink and rosemary-scented.

'Mmm, lovely lamb,' replies Maria, stalling for time and unsure of what to choose and where to start. She cuts into it enthusiastically, and with a hideous screech of knife on porcelain sends it skittering off the plate and into her lap.

'Easy, my dear. You'll find it's very tender. Cuts like butter.'

'Sorry.'

'My fault. I should have warned you.'

Maria wonders whether to lift it off her lap with her fingers, or whether a fork would be more appropriate. She watches helplessly as it slides down the crisp linen napkin and on to the stone-flagged floor.

'Sorry.' She dives after it.

'Just leave it. I'll pick it up later. For the cats. Have a bit more.'

Two more tender slices are slipped on to Maria's now dishevelled plate.

'What painters have been your most important influences?'

The lamb, going down, hits a sudden nervous knot, as Maria feels she's resitting her last art college finals. She chokes, splutters, almost recovers the morsel as it slips resolutely down the wrong way.

Catriona rises, strides round the table, seizes her from behind and thrusts her ribcage upward with a vigorous authority. The morsel shoots out of Maria's mouth and arcs delicately into a dish of sautéed wild mushrooms.

'Heimlich manoeuvre. Sorts it out every time.'

Maria, catching her breath, tries to lift the murderous mouthful out of the serving dish, so she can conceal it from view in her napkin, and manages to retrieve it while spilling her glass of wine all over the table.

'Oh God. I am so sorry.'

'Never mind, my dear, never mind,' beams Catriona warmly. 'It gives me the chance to show you a very neat trick.' She rises, disappears through a low, lintelled doorway on the far side of the baronial fireplace, Maria hears her footsteps clattering lightly down a spiral staircase, and soon Catriona reappears with a bottle of white wine. 'This will stand you in good stead for ever,' she remarks, uncorking it and pouring it with a theatrical gesture over the red-stained cloth.

Maria gasps.

'Don't worry, it's a completely insignificant little Muscadet that I keep for times like this. Now, you'll see that the white wine will completely neutralise the red, and the cloth will come up just fine. Once you know this, you need never feel embarrassed after a spill. And believe me, they can happen at the most awkward occasions, at the grandest dinner parties. It will save a fortune on cleaning bills. I think there's something fiendish about the way red wine always chooses to spill itself on to white fabric.'

'This is a lovely castle,' says Maria lamely, once things have settled down again. She is playing it safe and toying with a slice of delicately gratinéed potato.

'No it's not,' snaps Catriona. 'It is quite, quite hideous. But it's home. I can live here rent free. Which is why I can afford this not-bad claret. Have some more.' Ignoring Maria's gesture of protest, she pours the wine into the crystal glass.

'Has it been in your family a long time?'

'Since the heyday of that blond boy in the heavy gilt frame on the first landing.' Catriona tosses her head towards the stone staircase, lined with a gallery of ancestors who all appear to be glaring disdainfully at the dinner guest.

'And who is he?'

'That's Alasdair the Ambidextrous. Divided his favours more or less equally between his lady wife and King Jamie Stuart, taking them in turn on alternate week-nights. In grateful thanks he was awarded the castle, and the island along with it. There's a rude song about it in Gaelic that the local women used to sing while weaving the island tweed. But nobody can remember the second verse any more, which is a great pity, because it apparently said some things about the king's assumption of the English crown that would make your hair curl. Anyway, that's on father's side. On my mother's side the island stock goes back much, much further. Which did not endear Mama to her friends and neighbours, who always thought she was letting the side down by marrying the laird. Now, perhaps I could interest you in a little taste of cheese? There's another bottle I've decanted, from the same vintage but a different château. I thought you'd find the comparison interesting.'

'I don't really know much about wine,' says Maria apologetically, 'I think it would be wasted on me.'

Catriona sits upright, taps Maria smartly across the knuckles with her butterknife. 'Don't sell yourself short, woman. You're young enough to learn!'

She sweeps the serving platters and dinner plates away to an ancient oak sideboard, as long and heavy as a Victorian railway carriage, then returns with a board of cheeses and a fresh loaf of bread.

Maria nibbles morsels of unknown cheeses in nervous silence, waiting for the next phase of the inquisition, but Catriona, sniffing meditatively into her wineglass appears to have forgotten her existence.

Suddenly Catriona sits bolt upright, nailing Maria to her chair with a pointed, penetrating gaze. 'What you need,' she announces, seizing Maria's right hand and pulling it towards her, 'is your palm read.' Her grasp is strong, her fingers cool and silky. Maria stares, hypnotised, at the square-tipped fingers gently tracing curves and spirals over her palm.

'It's very clear to me that you have reached some kind of crossroads.'

'I'm sorry, but do you really believe in all this? I mean,

you being a doctor, and all, I would have thought ...'

'You know nothing about it,' snaps Catriona, 'but if you are going to be sceptical then I think there is no point in searching further. At least not for the moment.' She hands Maria her palm back. 'Coffee? We'll have it by the fire.'

'Oh, that would be lovely,' says Maria, rising with a sigh of relief and swiftly sending her empty wineglass flying as she does so. The crystal tinkles musically as it shatters on the stone. 'Oh, Christ. Oh Jesus, Mary and Joseph. Oh, Catriona, I am so sorry, I just don't know how I ... you must think I am a complete idiot ... I ...'

'On the contrary, my dear, it's been a most amusing dinner. You must not be so apologetic. It doesn't suit you. Anyway, I've always loathed this crystal. A birthday present from a very annoying second cousin. Perhaps if I invite you back next week, you'll do me an enormous favour and help me destroy the rest of the set.' Placing her hand firmly on Maria's nervously hunched-up shoulder, she steers her towards an overstuffed armchair by the fire. 'Now sit there, and I shall bring in the coffee. No, don't bother to help me. I'm really rather fond of this particular pair of cups and saucers. So do us both a favour, and just keep still.'

Sipping the coffee, freshly-ground and strong and fragrant, Maria begins to feel slightly dizzy. She thinks it's the wine, reaching her addled brain at last.

'Now, as I was saying,' says Catriona, settling into another deep chair on the other side of the fire, 'I am not going to let you leave here until you tell me more about yourself. Go on, sing for your supper.'

So Maria does. About light and colour and the problem of how to capture and create it when all the world about you is turning grey and flat and fogbound. About her early efforts at sculpture, and the scathing remarks of an instructor that sent her back to the comparative safety of paint and canvas. About her life in London and its recent, total disintegration. About her loss of her job, her self-confidence, and, worst of all, her creativity, for the fund of ideas and images has dried and shrivelled like a sloughed-off snakeskin in the sand, leaving her feeling empty, but riddled with guilt and frustration. She rouses herself from looking inwards, and wonders if Catriona is growing bored.

'Not at all,' says Catriona, smiling gently, her gaze continuing to flick lizardlike across Maria's face, and up and down her spare and anxious frame. 'But I think that it is high time you came to Cailleach. You almost left it too late.'

There seem to be four or five Catrionas sliding across her vision in a gentle dance. She wonders if her hostess has slipped something into the coffee, from an elegantly chased silver phial concealed in her black silk sleeve. She wonders if she will pass out, yet another mortification, and wake up to find herself en route to the brothels of Old Havana. ('Never take food from a stranger.' Her mother's long-ago warning rings like a bell across time.) Or, perhaps, in more classical vein, she will find herself transformed into a squealing pig, penned up in a sty with other bewildered ex-dinner guests. More likely, she decides, looking at the two bright pinpoints of firelight reflected in Catriona's steel-grey eyes, she will soon be lying on a baking tray on the scrubbed wooden table in the castle kitchen. Catriona will be pressing currants and bits of angelica into her body, just before she slips her into the ancient oven and bakes her into gingerbread.

'But first I'll have to fatten you up,' Catriona says softly.

'What?' says Maria, startled, sitting bolt upright.

'I said, I think it's time I drove you back to Ina's. It's getting late.'

Maria doesn't know whether to be relieved or disappointed, as her hostess helps her into her anorak.

From *The Fires of Bride*, published by The Women's Press

Mangiamania

Erika Ritter

It happened when I called up a friend to find out about her first date with a new man the night before.

'So how was it?'

'Terrific. We went to that new restaurant, the Italian place.'

'Sounds romantic.'

'No, Northern Italian, actually. The cuisine of Rome is spicier. This place has white sauces to die for and –'

'Wait a sec. What about your date?'

'Oh, he started with the *zuppa del giorno*, then moved on to –'

'No, what I'm asking is How did the evening go?'

'Not bad. Sixty bucks for two, including wine and tip.' Click.

As I hung up the receiver, I suddenly recalled how my

friend had met this new man. Over a tray of green pepper-
corns in a gourmet food shop. Somehow, it seemed
significant.

And what also seemed significant, now that I thought
about it, was the means by which three of my other friends
had recently met *their* new guys. One in a cooking course
titled 'French Without Fear'. Another while browsing
through a copy of *Gourmet* magazine in a bookstore. And
the third, reaching for the same package of *linguine verde* on
the grocery shelf.

Click. Click. Click.

Yes, something was definitely happening here. I decided
that a walk downtown would help me sort it all out.

Food, I realised, as I passed the fourth store window in
a row proclaiming a sale on wine thermometers and
lettuce driers, had completely taken over. The kind of
enthusiasm people used to pour into collecting stamps and
breeding chinchillas was now being squandered on *crème
anglaise* and red lettuce.

And that wasn't all. As I stopped for a moment outside
a love shop, where the red satin lips dangling in the
window had a 'Going Out of Business' sign pinned to
them, the full horror of the situation dawned on me. The
sensual thrill of erotica had been all but eclipsed by the
new mangiamania.

Well, damn it all, I thought. The old libidinous order
can't be allowed to just pass away. Not while there's breath
in this oh-so-willing body. I squared my shoulders and,
turning my back forever on lettuce driers, marched bravely
into the love shop.

L'Amour français was the promising title of the video
cassette I selected and carried home with me in the
deepening dusk.

Ah, what a treat. Curled up in bed with a lushly smutty
movie, devouring lustful images more eagerly than

champagne truffles from Fauchon ...

The film opened with a pouty young French man picking up a pouty young French girl on a wharf in Marseilles. Exactly *how* he picked her up, however, I failed to notice, because for some reason my interest was caught by all the fish strewn on the pier. I could just imagine them pan-fried with a soupçon of butter, and some freshly crushed garlic.

By the time I pulled myself back to the story line, the pouty French couple (I didn't catch their names, I was too busy watching them nibble flaky croissants from a *patisserie*) were back at his place, feverishly removing their clothes.

At that point, things got pretty hot and heavy – at least, I imagine they did. Unfortunately, my attention had been totally captivated by a still-life painting over their bed, featuring a neatly peeled Seville orange, some Anjou pears, a pomegranate (out of season), and a loaf of crusty bread, sprinkled with –

Click.

Trembling and furious with myself, I snapped off the set. What on earth was happening to me?

Frantic now, I rummaged in my dresser drawer for a novel I'd picked up in the drugstore a day or two before. Ah, here it was. *First Blissful Encounter*. Now, surely a chapter or two of that was all I needed to reaffirm that what I was looking for was the food of love, not vice versa.

Trying to feel confident, I opened the book on the first page. 'It all began,' I read, 'with a kiss from my companion.' Now that, I thought, was a very routine way for an evening to begin. And did they *both* have to start with the kiss? Couldn't her companion have ordered something different?

'At first,' the book went on, 'his caresses seemed bland.' Yes, I could imagine the kind of bland caresses her companion would serve up, seasoned without inspiration.

Fondly I cast my mind back to some truly outstanding kisses I had read about, kisses of the delectable sort available in the great European capitals, where the men not only make them spicy, but also totally fresh.

'At last, he took me in his arms, tenderly, delicately.' Good grief, I scoffed, you call *that* a hug? A hug should always be robust and full-bodied, and heated to such a temperature that it can completely melt any resistance that –

Oh my God. I slammed shut the covers of the book, the cold sweat pouring down my neck. Could it be that mangiamania had claimed another victim?

Striving to be calm, I padded out to the kitchen to see what I could find in the fridge. I don't know why, but I always think better with something to eat. A wedge of perfectly aged Gorgonzola, accompanied by fragrant muscat grapes, and perhaps a chilled glass of that incomparable Bordeaux that everyone is ...

From *Urban Scrawl*, published by Macmillan Canada

Red, White and Absolutely Blue

Lesléa Newman

You want to know why I'm eating blue spaghetti with tomato sauce and tofu all by myself on the Fourth of July? There's a simple, logical, one-word explanation: Margaret.

She left me. I was looking forward to spending a whole day with her smack dab in the middle of the week. You know, we'd get up late, make love, hang out, drink coffee, go back to bed, have a picnic, watch the fireworks. Well, that was the plan, but it seems my Margaret was off somewhere making fireworks of her own. With someone else. And like a poorly written soap opera, I was the last to know.

So, while the rest of Boston was celebrating the birth of our nation (or protesting it, whatever turns you on) I was alone. All by myself with no picnic ingredients, no party to go to, no one to ooh and aah with down at the

Esplanade when it got dark and they shot those babies up into in the air.

So, I moped around most of the day feeling sorry for myself, and then at about five o'clock I snapped out of it. I mean, I had no right to fall into the pity pot. I was young, healthy, employed and reasonably good looking, with a roof over my head and food on the table. That's when I decided, what the heck, I'd make myself a festive meal and have a private celebration. Hell, I'm a woman of the nineties. I don't need anyone else, right? I can take care of myself.

So, due to the day being what it was, and me being the cornball that I am, the meal had to be red, white and blue. I opened the refrigerator and immediately saw red: a jar of Paul Newman's tomato sauce. Perfect. Red was for blood, anger, revenge, how dare that bitch leave me for somebody else? I'm the best thing that ever happened to her. And she knew it, too. Or used to know it.

Now I was feeling blue. Blue food was trickier. I didn't have any blueberries in the fridge. On to the pantry. Would navy beans count? Hardly. How about a can of green beans? Almost, but not quite. Although some people have trouble telling the difference between blue and green and some people don't even think there is a difference. I found that out a few years ago when I was waiting for the 'T' at Harvard Square. A music student from Japan struck up a conversation with me, pointing at my sweater with her flute case. 'That's a nice green sweater,' she said, though my sweater happened to be blue. When I told her that, she smiled and said there was only one word for blue and green in Japanese, which sounded quite lovely and meant the colour of the water. I started wishing my subway would never come, but of course it did, and off I went, only to meet Margaret three days later as a matter of fact. But I refuse to think about that now.

Anyway, the point is, if I was Japanese, the green beans would do just fine, but then again, if I was Japanese, I'm sure I wouldn't give a flying fuck about the Fourth of July.

Back to the pantry. That's when I spotted those little bottles full of food colouring: red, green, yellow and blue. I'd gotten them last year for St Patrick's Day, to make bona fide green mashed potatoes for Margaret. The blue bottle was still full. What could I dye with it?

Why, spaghetti, of course. We used to colour spaghetti when I taught day care. We'd save this special activity for a freezing Friday in February when the kids were off the wall from being cooped up all week, and the teachers were going bananas from five days of dealing with seventeen pairs of mittens, boots, snow pants, scarves, sweaters, hats and jackets. To while away the afternoon, we'd cook up a huge vat of spaghetti, dye it different colours and throw it against the wall, where it would stick, making a mural I'm sure Picasso himself would have been proud of.

I put up a pot of water, contemplating blue: sadness, an ocean of tears, Lady Day singing the blues, red roses for a blue lady, that was me all right. Sigh.

Two down and one to go. White. Like every good dyke, I didn't have any white bread, white flour, white sugar or white rice in my cupboard, but I did have that handy dandy item that no lesbian household is complete without: a virgin block of tofu sitting on the top shelf of the refrigerator in a bowl of water. I chopped it up, thinking about white: a blank page, empty space, *tabula rasa*, clean sheets, starting over, yeah.

So I set the table and sat down with my very own red, white and blue meal, feeling angry, empty and sad. To tell you the truth, the plate in front of me wasn't very appealing. I took a bite anyway and swallowed. Not too bad, actually. A little chewy maybe, but other than that, okay. After I forced four bites down past the lump in my throat, it hit me: it wasn't just the Fourth of July I was celebrating; it was Independence Day. I was celebrating my independence by eating a completely ridiculous meal and the best part about it was I didn't have to explain it or justify it or defend it or hide it or even share it with anyone. I tell you, the fifth bite was delicious, and after that the food just started tasting better and better. As a matter of fact, I don't remember spaghetti ever tasting so good. I had seconds and then thirds. I ate it with my fingers, I let the sauce drip down my chin, I picked up the plate and licked it clean. Yum, yum, yum. My country 'tis of me.

From *Every Woman's Dream*, published by New Victoria Publishers

Hot Chicken Wings

Jyl Lynn Felman

Esther wanted silence. It had been eight hours since she had met Channah and Saul in the AIR FLORIDA terminal for their flight to Jamaica, and Esther was afraid she wasn't going to last the whole ten days. She had waited months for this reconciliation. But growing inside her was the terrible feeling that she needed to be saved from her very own parents. Then she laughed out loud. Maybe it was really Channah and Saul who needed to be saved from her, their very own daughter.

Esther took the elevator down to the lobby of the Windsor Hotel. Walking out the back door, she found herself in the middle of a pink patio, hot-pink lounge chairs everywhere. Nothing was familiar. She was used to the Piccolo Porch, to all the Jews sitting in brown wicker chairs at the Doral Hotel in Miami Beach, reading the

Jewish Daily Forward and arguing about Polish solidarity.

The sun reflected a glaring light on the patio, but Esther couldn't stop staring at the pink plush. Her white cheeks burned. She had to close her eyes. With her eyes shut tight Esther's mind snapped into focus and she understood the problem with the pink. It just wasn't real. Staying here, right in front of the ocean, with the cool breeze coming in off the water, piped-in reggae music, fried plantain and tropical drinks served all day poolside definitely made her a tourist.

But Channah said they should try some place new, different; to give the family another chance, Esther hoped. They could never have reconciled in Miami Beach. There were too many relatives and family friends wanting to know what's what all the time. So they had come to Jamaica.

Esther's family on her mother's side were descendants of Sephardic Jews who had settled in Montego Bay when the Jews were expelled from Spain. As she grew up Esther learned that the Caribbean had always been a haven for Jews, sometimes the only place that would take them in.

She knew her parents rarely travelled outside the US; neither her father nor her mother felt safe anywhere the Jews had been expelled or exterminated. To date, Channah and Saul had been to Israel, the Anne Frank house in Amsterdam and Miami Beach. It had been a risk to fly to Jamaica, but her mother felt as though the family were returning home. So, okay, maybe she was only half a tourist.

'Hello, darlin. Welcome to Jamaica.' Quickly Esther turned away from the hot-pink lounge chairs and opened her eyes.

'Charlotte Loudon, here.' Charlotte was smiling a huge smile. Esther tried to smile back. She reached instead for the Jewish star hanging between her breasts.

'Esther Pearl Friedman. I'm with my parents, we came here to talk.'

Charlotte wasn't just smiling. She was grinning from behind her eyes. But Esther could barely meet her smile, even though it was the smile itself she craved. Charlotte was dressed in a uniform. A green military blouse covered her large round breasts. She wore a tight, khaki-coloured skirt, short above the knees, with black ankle socks and black tie shoes.

'Are you the tour guide?'

'Man, I guard di door rite here at di Windsor Hotel.' The woman was laughing in Esther's face.

Esther thought fast. She knew she couldn't spend all ten days with her parents, no matter how much she'd missed them over the last seven months. She took a deep breath before pleading softly. 'I want to travel with you.'

'Dat okay wid me, honey. When yuh want see mi beautiful country?'

'As soon as possible, I mean it ... and Charlotte ...' Esther swallowed hard before whispering into the big smile, 'I go with girls.'

'Girls fine wid me, mi luv.' The guard reached out for Esther's hand. She had a firm grip. 'Check me later, darlin. Ah be waitin.'

'Esther!' Channah walked out into the pink patio just as Esther's hand met the hand of the woman in the khaki-coloured skirt who was already turning around, walking towards the hotel lobby.

'Who was that?' Channah wanted to know.

'My tour guide.'

'Esther Friedman, you don't need a tour guide in Montego Bay. We came here for the sun. To say *Kaddish* for our family. And to talk.'

'I need a tour guide wherever I am.' Esther needed patience. It had only been a year since she had told her parents the wonderful news that she loved women. 'I'll meet you for dinner – just tell me what time.' Esther understood her parents' disappointment. Not one of their three daughters had turned out according to the family plan. Her parents felt they deserved better than a divorce from an assimilated French Jew and a marriage to a Freudian psychiatrist who didn't believe in standing under the *chupah*. The problem was that her parents didn't understand Esther's disappointment with them.

'Seven o'clock, sharp. We'll wait for you in the lobby.' Esther tried to meet her mother's eyes, but when she did, all she saw was the flash of her mother's pain moving across her face. She wanted to hug Channah, to tell her she was glad they came to some place new. But she was afraid Channah wouldn't hug her back. Instead she nodded, turned around and walked back into the hotel, wondering which door Charlotte was guarding now.

Esther stood alone in front of the elevators. When the doors opened, Charlotte walked out, almost bumping into Esther.

'Estie, where yuh been keepin yuh sweet self?' The gold in Charlotte's teeth caught her eyes.

'When does the tour begin?'

'Tomorrow mi day off.' Charlotte's whole body smiled when she spoke. Her feet tapped the hotel floor lightly. Esther felt the smile coming up through the earth itself. By tapping her foot, Charlotte returned what she borrowed. 'Why yuh head so busy, man?'

'I was just watching you live.' Esther winked at Charlotte. 'So tomorrow's our day. What'll we do?'

'Whatever yuh want, sweet Estie. Mi coming early, so we have di whole day.'

'I want to eat Jamaican.' Esther decided to take advantage of vacationing – for the first time in her life – beyond the brown wicker chairs of Miami Beach.

'Sure darlin, Ah go cook. Wear yuh walkin shoes. We walkin far to mi house from di bus. Catch yuh later, dis hotel need a guard.' After a quick nod goodbye, Charlotte walked away.

Alone in the elevator, Esther tried to understand what she wanted from this trip. She knew she had longed for her family. But she didn't miss the heartache that always followed being together as family, as Jews. Even studying at Brandeis where most of the students were Jews and she was majoring in Judaic Studies, hadn't brought back that warm feeling of belonging to her people. Crowds of heterosexual Jews made her feel worse.

It was only Sunday. She told herself to take one day at a time, hour by hour if she had to.

At seven sharp Esther met her parents in the hotel lobby. They walked towards her just like two ordinary human beings. Everyone had dressed for the evening. Channah had on her favourite skirt-and-blouse ensemble. Esther had to admit her mother had good taste; the material was a soft silk, light blue and sea green. Channah's face was already tanned. Saul wore his summer suit, without a tie. He smiled at Esther.

'Where are we going for dinner?' Esther's voice was friendly.

'The Montego Bay Beach and Tennis Club, it's just up the road and comes highly recommended in the *Kosher Traveler*,' Channah answered, not looking at Esther and not looking away, just looking.

Channah and Saul walked out the Windsor in front of Esther. They formed a perfect triangle. Esther remembered her therapist always said to stay away from triangles, only Esther had thought she meant love triangles, but now she knew that any triangle was dangerous, and that there was no way out, but physically to step out. Besides, a triangle was only half a Jewish star.

Saul asked the bellman to get a cab. Esther felt a large movement behind her. Charlotte.

'Yuh parents dese, sweet darlin?' Esther reeled around, hostile, until she realised no one had heard the love talk but Esther and Charlotte. Esther coughed.

'These are my parents, Saul and Channah Friedman.' She knew her mother expected to be introduced.

'You're Esther's new friend, aren't you?' Channah said. Charlotte grinned. Esther didn't say a word.

'Cab's here.' Saul called out. Charlotte walked with them.

For a minute Esther imagined she was going to bend down and step right into the cab with her parents. But she didn't.

The cab pulled up at a giant ranch. As soon as they walked into the dining room, which was like an old cowboy movie – big round tables in huge circles circling a gigantic fireplace – Esther knew her mother was going to say that the dining room was a little too much. Saul looked around before making his announcement, 'Not many of us in here.'

'That's exactly what I was thinking.' Channah looked at Esther for support. Esther knew her parents were uncomfortable in the strange *goyishe* dining room and so was she.

Esther wondered about her mother's relatives; they had all been small shopkeepers and members of the United Congregation of Israelites. She couldn't picture anyone in her family sitting down to eat in a place like this. She wished her relatives were still alive so she could talk to them about being outsiders in beautiful Jamaica. Esther looked at her parents; she knew they longed for the *Jewish Daily Forward* and Miami Beach, where everybody drank iced tea from short, wide rimmed glasses and played bridge for hours. For a moment, they were a family again.

But Esther couldn't stop thinking about Charlotte. Where was she? What was she having for dinner? Was she with her lover? ... Esther closed her eyes to see better: she felt the warmth of two big women sprawled out on a tiny double bed, feeding each other and laughing as the food spilled on to the sheets. Esther decided to have the fresh local tuna. She had read in *National Geographic* that it was a Jamaican fish.

She knew that tuna was *kosher*; the mothers didn't eat their young or prey off other fish. Esther had always hated the image of a mother eating her children. Whenever she smelled *treyf* she immediately saw the floor of the ocean in her head. She pictured big shrimps, scallops, and giant oysters devouring their babies and any other fish swimming in their path.

Keeping kosher had always been important to Esther. When she was thirteen, right after her *Bat Mitzvah*, Esther had immersed herself in the meaning of *kashrut*, in hallowing the very act of eating. It was a way for Esther to eat with Jews everywhere and have Jews everywhere eat at her table.

She closed her eyes, wishing that she was alone with Charlotte. Esther hadn't remembered how depressing it was to be with her parents. She had always wanted an adult relationship with Saul and Channah. *Well, here it is*, she told herself. Then she had to put her fork down and stop eating. 'I'm going to the bathroom, the waiter can take my plate.'

She looked at herself in the mirror, shaking her head, not wanting to believe that absolutely nothing had changed. She knew her parents were unhappy. They had told no one, not even Rabbi Jacobson that their baby wanted their blessing to bring home a Sabbath bride instead of a groom. So no one had brought up her life; no one had even asked her if she was happy.

Being a lesbian made life with Channah and Saul so difficult. Her mother had stopped inviting her home for the holidays, and Saul had specifically said they weren't interested in any details, not even Esther's new friends. She could still hear Channah's reaction to her good news: *But why did you have to go and spoil everything? Why tell us?* Esther knew then, that the only way into the Friedman family was to be like Channah and Saul. There really wasn't anything to talk about. Esther returned to the table. She looked straight at her parents for the first time since arriving on the island. 'I want dessert. Is anyone going to join me?'

'We'll split something with you,' Channah said.

'No, I want my own.' Esther shut her eyes and waited. Nothing happened. When the waiter came back she ordered Baked Alaska because she had always loved the taste of the meringue on her tongue as it melted.

Saul paid the bill while Esther took a last look at the big round tables. She was back at Camp Ramah, sitting with hundreds of young campers, cutting their *kosher Shabes* chicken breasts simultaneously. She stood to bless the wine, surrounded by over two hundred and fifty adolescent Jewish voices, singing as though their voices alone could call the prophet Elijah back to Earth. That was the last time Esther really felt at home.

Of course it never happened that the entire Camp Ramah dining room began eating at the exact same moment, but Esther used to fantasise every *Shabes*, that all her people everywhere, were striking matches as the sun set, welcoming in the weekly festival. In her mind for one brief moment, she had brought peace to the Jews, and to her family. Finally, Esther had to admit that being Jewish and being a Friedman weren't the same thing.

'Estie, Estie!' Charlotte was waving her hands and calling to Esther. But it didn't look like Charlotte at all.

Her green military blouse and khaki-coloured skirt were gone. Instead, she wore a purple beret balanced just above her left eyebrow. Deep red rouge was smoothed into brown skin; red lip gloss wet her mouth. Charlotte had hooped gold earrings, two and three, in each ear.

'Ya *finally* ready, man?' Esther nodded, following her out the lobby of the Windsor Hotel and down the road to the bus stop. In the hot sun, Charlotte's black pants shined and her white blouse looked like silk. She carried a red and green, hand-woven pouch and a small, brown paper bag in her left hand.

Charlotte's legs moved fast on the gravel road. Esther had to run to keep up. This was a new Charlotte, quick, taking up space. On the bus, Charlotte sat down, stretched her legs out across an entire seat, and said hello whenever someone she knew walked by. Esther sat alone in the row directly behind Charlotte.

By the time they reached downtown, Charlotte was asleep and Esther's eyes were wide open. The bus stopped inside a huge open market decorated in banners of gold, green, shiny black and red. In booth after booth people sold food, clothes, records. The smells — red onions, ripe mango, salt fish — blended together, making Esther sick. Charlotte woke up and motioned for Esther to follow her.

They walked across the street to another bus stop, and waited ten minutes. They sat again in separate rows, as if they knew, without speaking that both of them needed a lot of space before their afternoon together. Pulling against the force of gravity, the bus climbed straight up into the Jamaican hills, while the town below got smaller and smaller.

Skinny, bone-thin dogs ran everywhere; the driver kept his hand on the horn. A baby lay crying right in the middle of the road, sprawled out on all fours, trying to crawl to the other side. The bus circled around the screaming infant. As the bus climbed up, the temperature rose inside. Esther was hot. Everywhere there were trees, large wide-leafed palm trees reaching out, shielding the villages and the people.

Green, all shades; Jamaica was divided into shades of dark, light and yellow greens. From the window, the Jamaican green reminded Esther of Israel; slowly, she let in the yellow green Jamaican hillside. But she heard her father's voice in her head, like a tape recorded message playing over and over again: *Israel is the most beautiful country in the whole world.*

'Okay, Estie. Me stop dis.' Charlotte hadn't spoken for at least twenty minutes; Esther didn't recognise her voice, but she felt them rise in unison, a pair of woman-bodies bending and rising together in dance. 'Ready for some walking?' Charlotte looked at Esther for the first time since picking her up at the Windsor.

'What's in your bag?' Esther asked.

'Our supper, man. I went to di butcher dis morning for some chicken, wings and legs.' Charlotte was impatient. Esther didn't say a word; how could she explain the laws of *kashrut* to Charlotte?

Even though she wanted to eat Jamaican, she hadn't planned to eat *treyf.* She never ate meat in restaurants unless it had been ritually slaughtered and blessed. Out of respect for her people, and for the food itself, Esther separated the *kosher* from the un*kosher*, the holy from the unholy, and ate only what was permitted by Jewish law. When she ate, Esther belonged to Jerusalem.

'Mi children waitin ... Estie, pick up yuh feet.'

'Kids?'

'Yah man, mi have children, one boy and two pretty pretty little girls, brown and pretty.' Esther didn't think she heard right; this was the first time Charlotte had said anything about kids.

'Charlotte, you got a husband?'

Charlotte nodded, her purple beret moved up and down. They walked side by side now; their buttocks moving from right to left, hitting each other slightly because they were walking up hill while their bodies pulled them down. 'Mi man come and go; him workin in Miami Beach most time. Him send me a letter before him come home.'

'What about your woman?' Esther concentrated on walking straight up hill. Charlotte didn't owe her any explanations. For a second, Esther wondered if Charlotte's husband worked at the the Doral Hotel in Miami Beach; she couldn't bring herself to ask.

'Oh yes, darlin, when mi man travelling, mi and mi woman Caroline go to bed and have we a sweet time. Sometimes we don't get up for a whole day, just to feed the children and den we meet again.' They were almost at the top of the hill.

'Mi man love me, Estie. Mi have his picture at mi home. You'll see, girl.' Charlotte pointed to a path off the dirt road. They headed straight down the side of the hill, into the overgrown weeds, bushes and very green trees.

Holding back a big yellow-green bush, Charlotte showed Esther where to walk. As she moved forward, the same odour Esther always smelled on her body whenever she was afraid came up to her nose. The path wasn't cleared well and the brush scratched her legs. They climbed down, deep into the underbrush; the deeper they went, the greener the leaves became, the stronger Esther's body smelled.

Looking up, she saw that Charlotte had taken them way off the main dirt road. They stood in the middle of a row of small wooden huts. Walking over to the far end, they stopped in front of a silver tin door. Esther heard voices. Out of the bushes came a young boy as Charlotte whistled long and slow.

'Where di rest of di children?' Charlotte bent down to the size of her son, whispering and kissing inside each of his ears. 'Dem wid Caroline?" The boy nodded, standing almost at attention, watching Esther. His mother's eyes were in him.

'Let we go.' Charlotte nodded towards the door.

The hut was a single room, as big as her Windsor closet and bathroom combined. In the centre of the room was a double bed; Charlotte sat herself at the head. The boy jumped up, circling his mother with his body, protecting her. Esther stood in the doorway taking in all the Jamaican landscape never mentioned in the travel brochures.

To the right of the entrance was a big dresser with a mirror attached. Next to the dresser were several plastic milk cartons piled one on top of the other. From where she stood Esther could see dishes and silverware arranged in neat rows inside the milk cartons. On top of the cartons was a double gas burner. Everywhere, clothes were folded into neat piles.

The floor of Charlotte's house was made of firmly packed brown dirt. A broom was in the left corner by the doorway, and a dust pan. The only window was on the wall opposite the bed. The frame was empty, but the green from outside grew up around the glassless hole, filling it with a thick green softness.

'Estie, si–down, yuh rude girl; dis mi home.'

Charlotte cooked. She poured water from a jug on the floor into a saucepan and added a cup of uncooked rice. She made a work space on the bed by propping up a six by twelve wooden board with two bricks at each end. Taking the chicken parts out of the bag she had carried since early that morning, she separated the legs from the wings, making two piles, dipping and rolling each piece into a flour mixture. After flouring each piece, Charlotte covered the chicken with spices. Esther watched, trying to figure out what the great rabbis would tell her about eating Charlotte's unclean food.

Charlotte lit the burner. She poured oil into a frying pan, waited a few minutes, watching the oil sizzle and get hot. Then one by one, she placed the wings into the hot pan, stopping for only a second to stir the rice. Every few minutes she added spices, red, black and green powders to the hot oil. When she was done frying the wings, she started over with the legs. Charlotte's love went straight into the frying pan and into the steaming rice.

On the edge of the bed, Charlotte spread out a single straw mat painted red, filled one plate with hot rice and fried chicken wings then put it on the mat in front of Esther. 'Eat.'

'I don't want to eat alone.'

'Where yuh manners, girl? Jus eat.'

Esther picked up the fork. What did it mean that she was about to eat Jamaican chicken wings and rice? She reminded herself that she had arranged this day, she had made the date with Charlotte and even told her she wanted to eat Jamaican. So Esther put some rice on the end of her fork, added a piece of chicken and brought the fork slowly up to her mouth. She was eating Charlotte's wings, *treyf* and unclean that they were.

The food had lost its heat, but when Esther put it in her mouth, she tasted all the Jamaican spices that Charlotte had added while she cooked. Spices Esther couldn't see by looking at the cooked food. She had to taste them to know that they were actually red hot and sweet all in the same bite. Like nothing she had ever tasted before.

Esther chewed. The spices were overpowering. This wasn't the first time that Esther had ever eaten *treyf*, but in the past, whenever she brought unclean food to her lips, she had never been able to enjoy it as she did now. She remembered the first time she made love to a woman.

That was the beginning. Esther had been afraid to bring her tongue down between Judith's legs. She had spent a long time kissing arms, shoulders, eyes and face.

Finally there was nothing left to do but bring her wet tongue straight down Judith's breasts, stomach and inside her thighs. Those first woman smells had been overpowering too, sweet and hot like Jamaican spices. When her tongue circled between Judith's small thighs, Esther told herself to open her eyes and look at the curly mound of dark, black hair protecting her lover's vagina, but she had been afraid to look.

'Tasting is the same as looking,' Judith had said, reaching down to hold Esther's head close to her body. Esther had known she was right, so she let herself breathe in a little at a time, all the different smells hidden between Judith's legs. She remembered being surprised that the lips outside Judith's vagina had only a faint sweet smell. It was the inside that smelled strong and tasted so wet. Using her fingers to open Judith, Esther had to fight off the pious old Jew in her head. He was tearing apart a red, *treyf*, steaming lobster. Then slowly, as though praying, he dipped the white sweet, unholy fish into a pool of melted butter.

With her mouth inside Judith, Esther began to chew, taking small, gentle bites. Just as she was crossing over to join her lover, Channah and Saul pushed into her head. They stared at her, *their baby*, and Channah screamed, 'Go! Wash yourself until you're clean, don't come into my house with any of that filthy *treyf* on your tongue. Get rid of the smell before you walk into my kitchen.' Esther had had to stop, close her mouth before she gagged, and bring her head back up, next to Judith's.

They had held each other while Esther's whole body shook. But she wasn't shaking now. She was taking another bite out of Charlotte's sweet wing and thinking that all her life, she had been afraid of new, unknown and different spices, but now she was chewing bite by bite, Charlotte's crisp Jamaican skin.

'This is good. How do you get the flavours hot and sweet at the same time?' Esther piled more rice on her plate; stuffing her mouth full, she barely took time out to chew and swallow.

'Slow down, girl. Mi knows yuh eat rice before. Yuh eatin like yuh neva eat in yuh whole life.' Charlotte shook her head; her son was laughing.

'I feel like I haven't eaten for days, even weeks.' She was eating, really eating, almost as if for the first time. She laughed at herself. This then was Charlotte and Esther making love.

'Yuh want see some good pictures? I have one picture of me, mi man and Caroline.' Charlotte reached into another pile.

'Sure.' Esther talked with her mouth full. They sat on Charlotte's bed, her boy, Esther and Charlotte looking at family pictures. Esther had finished eating and all the kitchen equipment had been pushed aside; they were in the living room now.

'Dis one mi favourite, man. Everybody mi love and who love me be together lookin out at di world.' Charlotte handed Esther a picture with three adults standing in the middle of the road. They held each other, looping their arms together behind their backs. Esther knew without asking who was in the picture.

'That's mi woman Caroline, dere at di end, me in di middle and mi man Samuel on di other end.' Esther stared at the picture. Something was going on in there that Charlotte wanted her to see.

'Yuh done yet, wid yuh lookin at?'

Esther shook her head. Then she knew; it was in their bodies. If she looked closely at the way they stood, with their hips lightly touching and their thighs and knees bending into each other, Esther saw what Charlotte had been trying to tell her since they met. All three of them – Samuel, Charlotte and Caroline – were lovers. Esther steadied herself on the bed. She needed a few minutes to let in this new piece of truth, because it wasn't just about the three of them, living and loving in Montego Bay.

'So, you're all three together?'

Charlotte nodded.

'Anybody know besides me?'

'Impossible, sweet darlin. In Jamaica a person got to be either-or, Estie, not both. Dem say not enough room in di world for us to be both. But me, hate to choose; me want it all. Yuh di same, dem hungry eyes and dat dancin mouth, tell me right away. That's why mi bring yuh to mi home. Long time, I want someone from outside to talk to. So, I pick up mi sweet Estie.' Charlotte reached for the picture.

'I girl, mi separate in mi own beautiful country. Mi whole life, I needin to tell someone. Mi openin doors, lookin around, when I see yuh comin into di Windsor Hotel. I know den, mi found somebody doin what I do.'

So Charlotte was alone too, alone in green Jamaica. She had been eating unclean food, separate from her people, for years. Only she was doing just fine. It was Esther who had never learned that eating a little *treyf* was necessary to survive.

Esther had never been free to eat whatever she wanted, because that meant eating alone, without the Jews. Esther had always been afraid to eat by herself; once she started she might never stop. There were too many things to taste, like Charlotte and Caroline and Samuel all at once.

'I've got to leave, Charlotte.'

They looked at each other, closing out the boy, the hot chicken wings and rice, and the picture of Charlotte with her two lovers. Esther burned inside. This was only the second time in her whole life that she was full; the first time had been with Judith, her first woman lover. She had been unable to continue loving Judith like she wanted; every time she tried, she imagined her head turning into the red head of a steaming lobster whose antenna reached out to strangle her. But she didn't think that would happen anymore.

'I'll walk yuh to di bus.' Charlotte stood up.

They walked then, back up the green path, past all the other huts, and on to the road. When the bus came, Esther climbed the three steps by herself. In the centre of the open market where all the smells blended together, Esther walked off the bus. She took a deep breath, slowly breathing in the pungent blend of red onion, ripe mango and salt fish.

From *Hot Chicken Wings*, published by Virago

From A Piece of the Night

Michèle Roberts

Sunday morning, and the feast of the Assumption of the Blessed Virgin Mary into heaven. The principal festival of Barrières-sur-Seine, which holds the Virgin as its special benefactress.

Julie has insisted on cooking lunch for the traditional party after High Mass. She has begun to let herself enjoy French food again. She goes to the cellar to collect bottles of cider, dark green glass misted with cobwebs in the rack on the red-tiled floor. She wipes the bottles and sets them by the fireplace in the salon in readiness. She opens one, and pours herself a drink, wanting to recapture the russet taste, thin and pale gold it looks in the china cup, but sour and then suddenly warm in the stomach. She arranges pâté on a plate, and tastes a bit, earthy pork fat rolling on the tip of her tongue. She slices wide craggy tomatoes and furs them with parsley from the garden, she washes vegetables so fresh and muddy she feels the plot they grew in, sees the black woollen stockings of the widow Mévisse bending over her celery beds, edged with pebbles and scarlet lobelias. The paths dividing the garden's cornucopia into manageable neatness are of white gravel. Crunch crunch go the feet of Julie over them, white espadrilles on the white stones noisy as chewing sugared almonds at a christening party.

Julie has bought frozen chickens, sealed in plastic, from the village grocery shop. Ten years ago, this was a dark and cool place when you entered from the sun in the square outside, smelling of the small golden melons ripening in baskets, the different cheeses stacked on marble shelves in a low cupboard at the back. You proffer your black wire basket for it to be filled with eggs, you hold up an earthenware jar into which Madame Roland ladles fresh cream, thick and slightly sour. On Tuesdays, the fish-woman sets her baskets just outside, heaped with the greenblackblue of mussels, an extra person to chat to as you do your shopping. Today, the village store has a wide glass front, trolleys for self-service. Madame Roland has vanished into the back, busy with accounts; fewer people stop to shake hands with each other and enquire after the health of husbands and children.

Julie breaks the long baguettes into shorter sections so that they will fit into the bread drawer. The village has two bakeries, next door to each other, that compete for the custom of important families like the Fanchots. Long thin breakfast loaves collected every morning, heavier two-pound loaves bought later in the day as they emerge from ovens, galette for Sunday breakfast, brioche when there are visitors to tea, cakes collected after High Mass as a special dessert. Monsieur Fanchot père's favourite cake was always a species of éclair. Two round choux placed one on top of the other, the top one smaller, iced with brown-coloured cream, and surrounded with small brown tongues of cream. Monsieur Fanchot, anti-clerical, delights in explaining the joke to Julie and Claude every Sunday lunchtime. The cake is called a nun, he says gravely, you see the flames – she is burning in hell. Monsieur Fanchot has been dead for years, nonetheless Julie has bought a nun cake in his memory, and from the bakery currently favoured by her mother. She feels today it is important to honour family observances.

While she waits for the chickens to thaw, she begins on the sauce. Wine vinegar from the crock under the sink, hissing over a low flame, mixed with mace. Hot stock drips into eggs and cream. This is the food of her childhood, rich, and fresh, and varied. At Oxford she discovered English food: pork pies, fish and chips, bread pudding, yellow haddock for breakfast on Fridays. She is delighted by it, so different, the contempt of scholars for the mundane task of feeding bodies. They do not seem to notice what they eat, while on the other hand they eat as though starvation followed and preceded every meal. Eight am in the college dining-room, wedged between the hard brown chair and the long refectory table in a sisterhood of greed, hands reaching for a fifth slice of wet white toast to smear it with hoarded margarine concealed from late-comers under inverted cups, marmalade with rare strands of orange-peel caught in the clear jelly. Long thin sausages haloed in grease, cornflakes with white sugar snowed on top. The meal is served by women in green overalls who have been at work since seven. Silently they watch the intellectuals stuff themselves, unmade-up faces shining like the sausages, damp and rumpled clothes picked up from where they were thrown down the night before. The undergraduates leave mounds of debris on their plates; it is the work of other women to clear up after them.

Sister Veronica had explained food to her pupils at convent school. We eat in silence in order to remember Our Lord, the sacrifice of self, of body, that He made for us. We restrain ourselves from eating as much as we wish, from taking pleasure in food, lest we forget the heavenly food of His body and blood He offers us each Mass. Forget the hours of labour spent in the convent kitchen garden, the seasons of growth, of ripeness. Ignore the long work of preparation, the washing, scraping, shredding, boiling, the novices dissolving in the thick steam of mutton fat and boiling vats of custard. Call food a miracle instead, remember the loaves and fishes and praise Him, praise Him for carrots tasting of soap, dead ants in the dried apricots, the soggy puddings. Just as at home your mothers produce the miracle of three meals a day out of thin air and love, so here too, we the community say Grace and thank the Lord for all that He provides. Let us not forget we are a family in the convent, in our school. We learn to live together. Sudden loud noises, whether of pleasure or of grief, disturb our harmony, in the day as in the night. Praise be to Jesus sounding from every throat, in silence, lest our lips be tempted to linger on a morsel accidentally over-choice, to seek out other flesh than his.

Further back, further back. Claire holds me in her arms at times dictated by the book, the baby-bible. There is a special low chair, painted white, she wears a white linen apron, a smock that opens easily down the front. She has two of them, gathered from the yoke, one blue, with bunches of grey flowers, the other yellow, pink and blue, with painted wooden buttons. In later years she uses them as dust-covers for the fur coat and the fur cape hanging in her wardrobe. I begged for one of them when I was eighteen and the fashion for second-hand clothes began, I wore it proudly, never realising then why it became my favourite garment. I kept it hanging in my own wardrobe, I wore it again, when I was pregnant with Bertha, and when I was feeding her, and then I used it as a painting-smock, when I moved from Oxford to south London and painted the front door of the house bright gold.

To feed me is her duty; she has read the books which warn of my ill health and emotional deprivation if a bottle is used. She has no choice in the matter, her body is an instrument for the state, the factory where healthy workers breed. She does not care for the emotive side of breast-feeding, it is just a job. The correct amount, the correct length of time the baby sucks each breast. I do not understand that; this is my first love-affair, and I am demanding as all lovers are. She is my world, and I am hers, nothing else matters except exquisite pleasure, mine. She must do what I want, go on fulfilling me. Love is her duty: a mother gives and gives. I snatch at her fat breast, she winces. We glare at one another. Love is a battle now, between the two of us. I suck too eagerly, I choke on love and sweetness. Am I allowed to go at my own speed, am I allowed to suck to satiety? And why not? She feeds me when she, not I, decides I need it, because she, like me, does not recognise that there are boundaries between us. I am enraged, I kick and scream upon her lap, a difficult child to wean.

What I do can never please her, for she, like me, hungers for fulfilment, for perfection. All she is allowed to do is feed us. If we love her, we will eat. We go together to daily morning Mass, both of us begging God for food, more food. Neither of us, the ageing mother, the adolescent daughter, is much impressed with life for women after puberty. We concentrate instead on our eternal hopes. We swallow the Christ, who should be our sufficiency. We are two heretics who get up, sighing still with hunger, we turn away, until tomorrow when we can come back for more. The priest reads the Fathers of the Church on the voraciousness of women. We are just like beasts, wild beasts.

From *A Piece of the Night*, published by The Women's Press

The Remains of the Feast

Githa Hariharan

The room still smells of her. Not as she did when she was dying, an overripe smell that clung to everything that had touched her, sheets, saris, hands. She had been in the nursing home for only ten days but a bedsore grew like an angry red welt on her back. Her neck was a big hump, and she lay in bed like a moody camel that would snap or bite at unpredictable intervals. The goitred lump, the familiar swelling I had seen on her neck all my life, that I had stroked and teasingly pinched as a child, was now a cancer that spread like a fire down the old body, licking clean everything in its way.

The room now smells like a pressed, faded rose. A dry, elusive smell. Burnt, a candle put out.

We were not exactly roommates, but we shared two rooms, one corner of the old ancestral house, all my twenty-year-old life.

She was Rukmini, my great-grandmother. She was ninety when she died last month, outliving by ten years her only son and daughter-in-law. I don't know how she felt then, but later she seemed to find something slightly hilarious about it all. That she, an ignorant village-bred woman, who signed the papers my father brought her with a thumb print, should survive; while they, city-bred, ambitious, should collapse of weak hearts and arthritic knees at the first sign of old age.

Her sense of humour was always quaint. It could also be embarrassing. She would sit in her corner, her round plump face reddening, giggling like a little girl. I knew better than ask her why, I was a teenager by then. But some uninitiated friend would be unable to resist, and would go up to my great-grandmother and ask her why she was laughing. This, I knew, would send her into uncontrollable peals. The tears would flow down her cheeks, and finally, catching her breath, still weak with laughter, she would confess. She could fart exactly like a train whistling its way out of the station, and it gave her as much joy as a child would get when she saw, or heard, a train.

So perhaps it is not all that surprising that she could be flippant about her only child's death, especially since ten years had passed.

'Yes, Ratna, you study hard and become a big doctor, madam,' she would chuckle when I kept the lights on all night and paced up and down the room, reading to myself.

'The last time I saw a doctor, I was thirty years old. Your grandfather was in the hospital for three months. He would faint every time he saw his own blood.'

And, as if that summed up the progress made between two generations, she would pull her blanket over her head and begin snoring almost immediately.

I have two rooms, the entire downstairs, to myself now

since my great-grandmother died. I begin my course at medical college next month, and I am afraid to be here alone at night.

I have to live up to the gold medal I won last year. I keep late hours, reading my anatomy textbook before the course begins. The body is a solid, reliable thing. It is a wonderful, resilient machine. I hold on to the thick, hardbound book and flip through the new smelling pages greedily. I stop every time I find an illustration and look at it closely. It reduces us to pink, blue and white colour-coded, labelled parts. Muscles, veins, tendons. Everything has a name. Everything is linked, one with the other, all parts of a functioning whole.

It is poor consolation for the nights I have spent in her warm bed, surrounded by that safe, familiar, musty smell.

She was cheerful and never sick. But she was also undeniably old, and so it was no great surprise to us when she suddenly took to lying in bed all day a few weeks before her ninetieth birthday.

She had been lying in bed for close to two months, ignoring concern, advice, scolding, and then she suddenly gave up. She agreed to see a doctor.

The young doctor came out of her room, his face puzzled and angry. My father begged him to sit down and drink a cup of hot coffee.

'She will need all kinds of tests,' he announced. 'How long has she had that lump on her neck? Have you had it checked?'

My father shifted uneasily in his cane chair. He is a cadaverous looking man, prone to nervousness and sweating. He keeps a big jar of antacids on his office desk. He has a nine to five accountant's job in a government owned company, the kind that never fires its employees.

My father pulled out the small towel he uses in place of a handkerchief. Wiping his forehead, he mumbled, 'You

know how these old women are. Impossible to argue with
them.'

'The neck,' the doctor said, more gently. I could see he
pitied my father.

'I think it was examined once, long ago. My father was
alive then. There was supposed to have been an operation,
I think. But you know what they thought in those days. An
operation meant an unnatural death. All the relatives came
over to scare her, advise her with horror stories. So she said
no. You know how it is. And she was already a widow then,
my father was the head of the household. How could he, a
fourteen-year old, take the responsibility?'

'Well,' said the doctor. He shrugged his shoulders. 'Let
me know when you want to admit her in my nursing
home. But I suppose it's best to let her die at home.'

When the doctor left, we looked at each other, the
three of us, like shifty accomplices. My mother, practical
as always, broke the silence and said, 'Let's not tell her
anything. Why worry her? And then we'll have all kinds
of difficult old aunts and cousins visiting, it will be such a
nuisance. How will Ratna study in the middle of all that
chaos?'

But when I went to our room that night, my great-
grandmother had a sly look on her face. 'Come here,
Ratna,' she said. 'Come here, my darling little gem.'

I went, my heart quaking at the thought of telling her.

She held my hand and kissed each finger, her half-closed
eyes almost flirtatious. 'Tell me something, Ratna,' she
began in a wheedling voice.

'I don't know, I don't know anything about it,' I said
quickly.

'Of course you do.' She was surprised, a little annoyed.
'Those small cakes you got from the Christian shop that
day. Do they have eggs in them?'

'Do they?' she persisted. 'Will you,' and her eyes

narrowed with cunning, 'will you get one for me?'

So we began a strange partnership, my great-grand-mother and I. I smuggled cakes and ice cream, biscuits and samosas, made by non-Brahmin hands, into a vegetarian invalid's room. To the deathbed of a Brahmin widow who had never eaten anything but pure, home-cooked food for almost a century.

She would grab it from my hand, late at night after my parents had gone to sleep. She would hold the pastry in her fingers, turn it round and round, as if on the verge of an earthshaking discovery.

'And does it really have an egg in it?', she would ask again, as if she needed the password for her to bite into it with her gums.

'Yes, yes,' I would say, a little tired of midnight feasts by then. The pastries were a cheap yellow colour, topped by white frosting with hard grey pearls.

'Lots and lots of eggs,' I would say, wanting her to hurry up and put it in her mouth. 'And the bakery is owned by a Christian. I think he hires Muslim cooks too.'

'Ooooh,' she would moan. Her little pink tongue darted out and licked the frosting. Her toothless mouth worked its way steadily, munching, making happy sucking noises.

Our secret was safe for about a week. Then she become bold. She was bored with the cakes, she said. They gave her heartburn. She became a little more adventurous every day. Her cravings were various and unpredictable. Laughable and always urgent.

'I'm thirsty,' she moaned, when my mother asked her if she wanted anything. 'No, no, I don't want water, I don't want juice.' She stopped the moaning and looked at my mother's patient, exasperated face. 'I'll tell you what I want,' she whined. 'Get me a glass of that brown drink Ratna bought in the bottle. The kind that bubbles and makes a popping sound when you open the bottle. The one with the fizzy noise when you pour it out.'

'A Coca-Cola?' said my mother, shocked. 'Don't be silly, it will make you sick.'

'I don't care what it is called,' my great-grandmother said and started moaning again. 'I want it.'

So she got it and my mother poured out a small glassful, tight-lipped, and gave it to her without a word. She was always a dutiful grand-daughter-in-law.

'Ah,' sighed my great-grandmother, propped up against her pillows, the steel tumbler lifted high over her lips. The lump on her neck moved in little gurgles as she drank. Then she burped a loud, contented burp and asked, as if she had just thought of it, 'Do you think there is something in it? You know, alcohol?'

A month later, we had got used to her new, unexpected, inappropriate demands. She had tasted, by now, lemon tarts, garlic, three types of aerated drinks, fruit cake laced with brandy, bhel-puri from the fly-infested bazaar nearby.

'There's going to be trouble,' my mother kept muttering under her breath. 'She's losing her mind, she is going to be a lot of trouble.'

And she was right, of course. My great-grandmother could no longer swallow very well. She would pour the coke into her mouth and half of it would trickle our of her nostrils, thick, brown, nauseating.

'It burns, it burns,' she would yell then, but she pursed her lips tightly together when my mother spooned a thin gruel into her mouth. 'No, no,' she screamed deliriously. 'Get me something from the bazaar. Raw onions. Fried bread. Chickens and goats.'

Then we knew she was lost to us. She was dying.

She was in the nursing home for ten whole days. My mother and I took turns sitting by her, sleeping on the floor by the hospital cot.

She lay there quietly, the pendulous neck almost as big as her face. But she would not let the nurses near her bed. She would squirm and wriggle like a big fish that refused to be caught. The sheets smelled, and the young doctor shook his head. 'Not much to be done now,' he said. 'The cancer has left nothing intact.'

The day she died, she kept searching the room with her eyes. Her arms were held down by the tubes and needles, criss-cross, in, out. The glucose dripped into her veins but her nose still ran, the clear, thin liquid trickling down like dribble on to her chin. Her hands clenched and unclenched with the effort and she whispered, like a miracle, 'Ratna.'

My mother and I rushed to her bedside. Tears streaming down her face, my mother bent her head before her and pleaded, 'Give me your blessings, Pati. Bless me before you go.'

My great-grandmother looked at her for a minute, her lips working furiously, noiselessly. For the first time in my life I saw a fine veil of perspiration on her face. The muscles on her face twitched in mad, frenzied jerks. Then she pulled one arm free of the tubes, in a sudden, crazy spurt of strength, and the IV pole crashed to the floor.

'Bring me a red sari,' she screamed. 'A red one with a big wide border of gold. And,' her voice cracked, 'bring me peanuts with chilli powder from the corner shop. Onion and green chilli bondas deep fried in oil.'

Then the voice gurgled and gurgled, her face and neck swayed, rocked like a boat lost in a stormy sea. She retched, and as the vomit flew out of her mouth, her nose, thick like the milkshakes she had drunk, brown like the alcoholic coke, her head slumped forward, her rounded chin buried in the cancerous neck.

When we brought the body home – I am not yet a doctor and already I can call her that – I helped my mother to wipe her clean with a wet, soft cloth. We wiped away the smells, the smell of the hospital bed, the smell of an old woman's juices drying. Her skin was dry and papery. The stubble on her head — she had refused to shave her head once she got sick — had grown, like the soft, white bristles of a hairbrush.

She had had only one child though she had lived so long. But the skin on her stomach was like crumpled, frayed velvet, the creases running to and fro in fine, silvery rivulets.

'Bring her sari,' my mother whispered, as if my great-grandmother could still hear her.

I looked at the stiff, cold body that I was seeing naked for the first time. She was asleep at last, quiet at last. I had learnt, in the last month or two, to expect the unexpected from her. I waited, in case she changed her mind and sat up, remembering one more taboo food to be tasted.

'Bring me your eyebrow tweezers,' I heard her say. 'Bring me that hair-removing cream. I have a moustache and I don't want to be an ugly old woman.'

But she lay still, the wads of cotton in her nostrils and ears shutting us out. Shutting out her belated ardour.

I ran to my cupboard and brought her the brightest, reddest sari I could find: last year's Divali sari, my first silk. I unfolded it, ignoring my mother's eyes which were turning aghast. I covered her naked body lovingly. The red silk glittered like her childish laughter.

'Have you gone mad?' my mother whispered furiously. 'She was a sick old woman, she didn't know what she was saying.' She rolled up the sari and flung it aside, as if it had been polluted. She wiped the body again to free it from foolish, trivial desires.

They burnt her in a pale brown sari, her widow's weeds. The prayer beads I had never seen her touch encircled the bulging, obscene neck.

I am still a novice at anatomy. I hover just over the body, I am just beneath the skin. I have yet to look at the insides, the entrails of memories she told me nothing about, the pain congealing into a cancer.

She has left me behind with nothing but a smell, a legacy that grows fainter every day. I haunt the dirtiest bakeries and tea-stalls I can find every evening. I search for her, my sweet great-grandmother, in plate after plate of stale confections, in needle sharp green chillies deep-fried in rancid oil. I plot her revenge for her, I give myself diarrhoea for a week.

Then I open all the windows and her cupboard and air the rooms. I tear her dirty grey saris to shreds. I line the shelves of her empty cupboard with my thick, newly-bought, glossy-jacketed texts, one next to the other. They stand straight and solid, row after row of armed soldiers. They fill up the small cupboard in minutes.

From *In Other Words: New Writing by Indian Women*, edited by Urvashi Butalia and Ritu Menon, published by The Women's Press

Burn Sugar

M Nourbese Philip

It don't come, never arrive, had not – for the first time
since she leave, had left home; is the first, for the first time
in forty years the Mother not standing, had not stood over
the aluminum bucket with her heavy belly whipping up
the yellow eggs them and the green green lime-skin.
'People does buy cake in New York,' she say, the Mother
had said, 'not make them.'

Every year it arrived, use to in time for Christmas or
sometimes – a few time well – not till January; once it
even come as late as in March. Wherever she is, happen to
be, it come wrap up and tie up in two or three layers of
brown wrapping paper, and tape up in a Peak Freans tin –
from last Christmas – over-blacked black black from the
oven. And it address on both sides – 'just to make sure it
get there,' she could hear the Mother saying – in the

Mother funny printing (she could never write cursive she used to say). Air mail or sea mail, she could figure out the Mother's finances — whether she have money or not. When she cut the string she use to, would tear off the Scotch tape — impatient she would rip, rip off, rip the brown paper, prise off the lid, pause ... sit back on she haunches and laugh — laugh she head off — the lid never match, never matched the tin, but it there all the same — black and moist. The cake.

The weeks them use to, would pass, passed — she eating the cake, would eat it — sometimes alone by sheself; sometimes she sharing, does share a slice with a friend. And then again — sometimes when she alone, is alone, she would, does cry as she eating — each black mouthful bringing up all kind of memory — then she would, does choke — the lump of food and memory blocking up, stick up in she throat — big and hard like a rock stone.

She don't know — when she begin to notice it she doesn't know, but once she has it always, was always there when she open the tin — faint — but it there, undeniable — musty and old it rise up, an odour of mouldiness and something else from the open tin making she nose, her nostrils twitch. Is like it cast a pall over she pleasure, shadowing her delight; it spoil, clouded the rich fruity black-cake smell, and every time she take a bit it there — in she mouth — hanging about it hung about her every mouthful. The Mother's advice was to pour some more make-sure-is-good-Trinidad rum on it. Nothing help, it didn't — the smell just there lingering.

And then she know, she knew that something on its annual journey to wherever she happened to be, something inside the cake does change, changed within the cake, and whether is the change that cause the funny smell, or the journey, the travel that cause the change that cause the funny smell ... she don't know ...

It never use to, it didn't taste like this back home is what the first bite tell she – back back home where she hanging round, anxiously hanging about the kitchen getting in the Mother's way – underfoot – waiting for the baking to start –

'Wash the butter!' The Mother want to get her out of the way, and is like she feeling the feel of the earthenware bowl – cool, round, beige – the Mother push at her. Wash the butter, wash the butter, sit and wash the butter at the kitchen table, cover with a new piece of oilcloth for Christmas; wash the butter, and the sun coming through the breeze blocks, jumping all over the place dappling spots on she hand – it and the butter running competition for yellow. Wash the butter! Round and round ... she pushing the lumps of butter round with a wooden spoon.

Every year she ask the same question – 'Is why you have to do this?' and every year the Mother tell she is to get the salt out of the butter, and every year she washing the butter. The water don't look any different, it don't taste any different – if she could only see the salt leaving the butter. The Mother does catch she like this every year, and every year she washing the butter for hours, hours on end until is time to make the burn sugar.

Now! She stop. The Mother don't tell she this but she know, and the Mother know – it was understood between them. The coal-pot waiting with it red coals – the Mother never let she light it – and the iron pot waiting on the coal-pot, and the Mother waiting for the right time. She push her hand in the sugar bag – suddenly – one handful, two handful – and the white sugar rise up gentle gentle in the middle of the pot, two handfuls of white sugar rise gently ... she had never, the Mother had never let she do it sheself, but to the last grain of sugar, the very last grain, she know how much does go into the pot.

She standing close close to the Mother, watching the white sugar; she know exactly when it going change –

after she count to a hundred, she decide one year; another year she know for sure it wasn't going change while she holding her breath; and last year she close she eyes and know that when she open them, the sugar going change. It never once work. Every time she lose, was disappointed – the sugar never change when she expect it to, not once in all the years she watching, observing the Mother's rituals. Too quick, too slow, too late – it always catch she – by surprise – first the sugar turn sticky and brown at the edges, then a darker brown – by surprise – smoke stinging, stings her eyes, tears run running, down she face, the smell sharp and strong of burning sugar – by surprise – she don't budge, she stand still watching, watches what happening in the pot – by surprise – the white sugar completely gone leaving behind a thick, black, sticky mass like molasses – by surprise. If the pot stay on long enough, she wonder, would the sugar change back, right back to cane juice, runny and white ... catching she – by surprise.

The Mother grab up a kitchen towel, grabs the pot and put it in the sink – all one gesture clean and complete – and it sitting there hissing and sizzling in the sink. The Mother open the tap and steam for so rise up and *brip brap* – just so it all over – smoke gone, steam gone, smoke and steam gone leaving behind this thick thick, black liquid.

She look down at the liquid – she use to call it she magic liquid; is like it have a life of it own – its own life – and the cake need it to make it taste different. She glance over at the Mother – maybe like she need the Mother to taste different. She wonder if the Mother need her like she need the Mother – which of them was essential to the other – which of them was the burn sugar?

She stick a finger in the pot and touch the burn sugar; turning she finger this way and that, she looking at it in the sunlight turning this way and that, making sure, she make sure you don't drop any of the burn sugar on the floor; closing she eyes she closes them, and touching she touch she tongue with her finger ... gently, and she taste the taste of the burn sugar strong and black in its bitterness — it bitter — and she skin-up she face then smile — it taste like it should — strong, black and bitter it going make the cake taste like no other cake.

She hanging round again, watching and waiting and watching the Mother crack the eggs into the bucket — the aluminum bucket — and she dying to crack some in sheself — if she begged she got to crack a few but most of the time she just hanging, hung around watching and waiting and watching the Mother beat the eggs. Is like the Mother thick brown arm grow an appendage — the silver egg whisk — and she hypnotising sheself watching the big arm go up and down scraping the sides of the bucket — a blur of brown and silver lifting up, lifts the deep yellow eggs — their pale yellow frothy Sunday-best tulle skirts — higher and higher in the bucket. The Mother stop and sigh, wipe she brow — a pause a sigh, she wipes her brow — and she throw in a piece of curly, green lime-skin, add a dash of rum — 'to cut the freshness' — a curl of green lime-skin and a dash of rum. She don't know if the Mother know she was going to ask why, to ask her why the lime-skin — anticipating her question — or if she was just answering she own question, she don't know, but the arm continued, keep on beating as if it have a life of it own with a life of its own, grounded by the Mother's bulk which harness the sound of she own beat — the scrape, swish and thump of her own beat.

She watching the Mother, watches her beat those eggs — how they rise up in the bucket, their heavy, yellow beauty driven by the beating arm; she remember the burn sugar and she wonder, wonders if change ever come gently ... so much force or heat driving change before it. Her own change had come upon her gently ... by surprise ...

in the night of blood ... by surprise ... over the months them as she watch her changes steal up on her ... by surprise ... the days of bloodcloth, the months that swell up her chest ... by surprise ... as she watched watching the swelling, budding breasts, fearful and frighten of what they mean, and don't mean. There wasn't no force there, or was there? too old and ancient and gradual for she or her to notice as she watch the Mother and wait, waiting to grow up and change into, but not like – not like she, not like her, not like ... she watching ... the Mother face shiny with sweat shines, she lips tie up tight tight with the effort of the beating arm, lips held in tight and she wondering, wonders whether she, the Mother, have any answers ... or questions. Did she have any – what were they?

Nobody tell she but she hand over the bowl, the bowl of washed butter she pass to the Mother who pour off the water and put in the white sugar – granulated and white she add it to the lumpy yellow mass, and without a word the Mother pass it back to her. She hand too little to do it for long – cream the butter and sugar – her arm always grows too tired too soon, and then she does have to pass it back to the Mother. But once more, one more time – just before the Mother add the eggs, she does pass it back to her again for she to witness the change – surprise sudden and sharp all the way from she fingers right up she arm along she shoulder to she eyes that open wide wide, and she suck in her breath – indrawn – how smooth the texture – all the roughness smooth right out and cream up into a pale, yellow swirl. When she taste it not a single grain of sugar leave behind, is left to mar the smooth sweetness.

She want it to be all over now – quick quick, all this mixing and beating and mixing, but she notice the sound change now that the eggs meet the butter – it heavier and thicker, reminding her it reminds her of the Mother – she and the Mother together sharing in the Mother's sound.

She leans leaning over the bucket watching how the eggs and butter never want to mix, each resisting the other and bucking up against the Mother force. Little specks and flecks of butter, pale yellow in defiance, stand up to fight the darker yellow of the eggs them, and little by little they disappear until the butter give up and give in, yields – or maybe is the other way around – the eggs them give in to the butter. Is the Mother hand that win, the Mother's arm the victor in this battle of the two yellows.

The Mother add the dry fruit that soaking in rum and cherry brandy for months now, then the white flour; the batter getting thick thickens, stiffens its resistance to the Mother's hand, the beating arm, and all the time the Mother's voice encouraging and urging – 'Have/to keep/beating/all the/time' – the words them heavy and rhythmical, keeping time with the strokes. The batter heavy and lumpy now, and it letting itself be pushed round and round the bucket – the Mother can only stir and turn now in spite of she own encouragement – but she refuse to let it alone, not giving it a minute's rest.

The Mother nod she head, and at last she know that *now* is the time – time for the burn sugar. She pick up the jar, holding it very carefully, and when the Mother nod again she begin to pour – she pouring the Mother stirring. The batter remain true to itself in how it willing to change – at first it turn from grey to brown – just like me she think, then it turn a dark brown like she sister, then an even darker brown – almost black – the colour of her brother, and all the time the Mother stirring. She empty the jar of burn sugar – her magic liquid and the batter colour up now like she old grandmother – a seasoned black that still betray sometimes by whitish flecks of butter, egg and sugar, and the Mother arm don't stop beating and the batter turning in and on and over itself.

'How you know when it ready?'

'When the spoon can stand in it,' and to show what she mean, the Mother stick the spoon the batter and it stand up stiff stiff.

Her spoon like the Mother's now stood at attention – stiff and alone in its turgid sea of black. It announced the cake's readiness for the final change of the oven. Was she ready? and was it the Mother's cake she now made? Or her own? Just an old family recipe – the cake had no other meaning – its preparation year after year only a part of painting the house, oiling the furniture, and making new curtains on the Singer machine that all together went to make up Christmas. She had never spoken to the Mother about it – about what, if anything, the cake and the burn sugar might mean ...

It was its failure to arrive – the absence of the cake – even with its 'funny' smell that drove her to this understanding, this moment of epiphany as she now stood over her cheap, plastic bowl and watched the spoon. She looked down at her belly, flat and trim where the Mother's easily helped balance the aluminum bucket – not like, not like, not like her – she hadn't wanted to be like her, but she *was* trying to make the Mother's black cake, and all those buckets of batter she had witnessed being driven through their changes were now here before her – challenging her. And she *was* different – from the Mother – as different perhaps as the burn sugar was from the granulated sugar, but of the same source. Here, over this bucket – it was a plastic bowl – she met – they met and came together – to share in this old old ritual of transformation and metamorphosis.

The Mother would surely laugh at all this – all this fancy talk with words like 'transformation and metamorphosis' – she who had warned of change, yet was both change and constancy. 'Is only black cake, child, is what you carrying on so for?' she could hear the voice. They didn't speak the same language – except in the cake, but now the Mother was sitting looking at her make the cake.

'Look, Mammy – look, see how you do it – first, the most important thing is the burn sugar – the sweetness of the cake need that bitterness – you can't have black cake without it.' Mammy was smiling now,

'You was always a strange one.'

'Shut up, Mammy, and listen,' (gently of course) 'just listen – the burn sugar is something like we past, we history, and you know that smell I always tell you about?' Mammy nod her head, 'I now know what it is – is the smell of loneliness and separation – exile from family and home and tribe – even from the land, and you know what else, Mammy – is the same smell of – '

'Is only a cake, child – '

'The first ones – the first ones who come here rancid and rank with the smell of fear and death. And you know what else, Mammy? is just like that funny smell of the cake when I get it – the smell never leave – it always there with us –'

'Is what foolishness you talking, child – fear and death? Just make the cake and eat it.'

'But, Mammy, that is why I remember you making the cake – that is what the memory mean – it have to mean something – everything have to have a meaning – '

'Let me tell you something, girl,' Mammy voice was rough, her face tight tight – 'some things don't have no meaning – no meaning at all, and if you don't know that you in for a lot of trouble. Is what you trying to tell me, child – that it have a meaning for we to be here – in this part of the world – the way we was brought here? That have a meaning? No, child' – the voice was gentler now – 'no, child, you wrong and don't go looking for no meaning – it just going break you – '

'Mammy – '

But Mammy wasn't there, at least not to talk to. She looked down at the batter. The burn sugar she used was some she the Mother had made earlier that year, accompanied by the high-pitched whine of the smoke alarm. She had made the batter by hand, as much of it as she could, even adding the green green corkscrew of lime-skin, although according to Mammy 'these modern eggs never smell fresh like they suppose to – like those back home.'

When they were done she almost threw the cakes out. She had left them too long in the oven and a thick crust had formed around them; the insides were moist and tasted like they should – the bitter, sweet taste perfectly balanced by the deep, rich, black colour. But the crust had ruined them. Obviously she wasn't ready, and only the expense of the ingredients had prevented her from throwing them out immediately.

It was the Mother's advice that saved them. Following her instructions by phone she cut all the crusts off the cakes, then poured rum over them to keep them moist. She had smaller cakes now – not particularly attractive ones either, but they tasted like black cake should, and without that funny smell.

Was that hard crust a sign of something more significant than her newness at making the cake? Was there indeed no meaning to the memory, or the cake, or the funny smell? She wanted to ask the Mother – she almost did – but she knew the Mother would only laugh and tell her – 'Cake is for eating not thinking about – eat it and enjoy it – stop looking for meaning in everything.'

She thanked the Mother, lowered the receiver slowly and said to herself – 'You wrong, Mammy, you wrong – there have to – there have to be a meaning.'

Callaloo Soup

Jean Buffong

'Bow wow wow ... wheee wheee ... wow wow ... wooow.'

'Ringo – what noise you making in the place so eh?' I shouted, the same time looking out of the kitchen window towards where the dog was barking. As the fishermen were casting their net in the bay I half expected to see William passing on his way there though why the dog should bark behind I don't know. People say he is the biggest loupgarou in the place and animals have extra sense could be why. As I pushed my head out of the window to see who it was, I heard little Junny calling.

'Marning Miss Effie, Mammy say if you have callaloo to spare her, a twenty-five cents please.'

'Aye aaye Junny. Marning. Is you Ringo barking behind so, going on as if he don't know you?'

'Bow wow wow.' The dog continued barking at the

child. 'Ringo stop it! Mash Ringo. Stop that noise in the place. You suppose to be watch dog, who for you to bark behind you don't. Shut up. You going on as if you don't know Junny!'

'Come, Junny, come. Don't worry with that stupid dog.'

'Miss Effie, Mammy say if you have callaloo to spare her, a twenty-five cents please,' the child repeated.

'How come Joyce send you for callaloo so early, she going out?'

'Yes Miss Effie. She pick up a little load, she going to town to make a turn, then she might go to Grenville by Tanty Maureen. She want to cook the dinner before she go. I leave her grating coconut to cook a piece of coo-coo. She buy fish last night; she want the callaloo to go with the fish and coo-coo.'

'Coo-coo, whey Joyce get the cornflour?'

'We had some dry corn in the house she send Calvin up by Mr Morris yesterday to grind some.'

'Aaye you in ting girl. Coo-coo, callaloo and fish for dinner!' I teased the child. She laughed.

I took a small knife and went behind the kitchen to the callaloo patch, Ringo following me. It was only Thursday so I couldn't cut too much callaloo because I knew by Saturday other people would be coming to buy and I also wanted two leaves for myself – you can't sell everything and leave your belly empty. When my granddaughter came from England last year and see me selling the little things around the house she laughed. She said I could open a little business. She use some big word saying I could be one of them. I don't know about that, you have to try any little thing to make a living ... a little callaloo, sieve, thyme, a pumpkin, any little thing.

Look at Joyce, this girl is something. She turn her hand to anything to look after her children, Junny and Calvin. She always saying she don't know if God will give her anymore. Junny say she had a load. I'm sure when the overseer came down yesterday she followed him up in the estate to buy oranges, mandarin and whatever she could find up there to go to town. I know she was keeping her eyes on the bunch of plaintain she have behind the house; it just started to turn. She could make a good sale of the plaintain, with some oranges, mandarin, cucumber and other little things, especially as the Trinidad boat coming in this morning. Joyce have sweet mouth; she know how to draw customers. Look how quick she does sell out her souse by the road. She used to make it only when there is dance in the big school, she doing such good business now she can't wait until there is a dance every Saturday evening, she in the fore road with the pan of souse, before you could cut your eyes she finish selling. Mind you is not only sweet mouth she have you, she hand just a sweet. Is not everybody could make a pig souse to taste good no matter what they put in it. Joyce knows exactly how much seasoning to use and how long to leave it on the fire to cusermeer; when it finish cooking she cut up some cucumber and put in to give it better taste. Those young boys and them say Joyce souse put water in their back; give them stamina. Stamina to interfere with those young girls instead of looking for work to do – damn scamps.

'And Miss Effie Mammy say if you have strong pepper, to send her one please.'

'Awright Junny awright.'

I cut some callaloo leaves, picked about three hot pepper, put them in a paper bag and handed them to the child. 'Tell Joyce to send a piece of the coo-coo for me, eh.'

'Awright Miss Effie. Thanks.'

As she made her way across the little track back to her house Ringo danced along in front as if he showing her the way home.

The sun was slowly staking its claim over the mountain.

The cool morning breeze had taken its leave. It was going to be one of those hotter than hot days. It rained for most of the night; in the morning everything was fresh and clean as though God send the rain to wash away yesterday's dirt. This December there's not so much rain, the days seem hotter than all other December, and the place so dry. It's a good thing the drain from the kitchen run into the callaloo patch keeping it from drying up.

'Miss Effie oye, marning. I see Junny come for callaloo early,' my neighbour Miss Elizabeth's oldest daughter, Rita, called out to me.

'Aye, marning Rita, marning. Girl, I think Joyce going in town early. She cooking before she go.'

I left the window from where I was watching Junny and Ringo dawdling along the little road and went to the back of the house to talk to her. Rita was sweeping around her house under the window in boundary by my sugar apple tree by the side of the callaloo patch. Half of the sugar apple tree was hanging over Rita yard so she always have to be cleaning up the dried leaves. I told them they could cut off the overhanging branches if it's a nuisance but they leave it because they pick the sugar apple when it ready.

'You ding hear that rain last night,' she said. 'I thought was Manuel throwing gravel on the window trying to wake my sister Judy. When I listen good good to the tin tink tingling I realise was grain of rain that falling on the galvanise.'

'What you mean Manuel throwing stone to wake your sister. Your mother not home!' I was a bit curious. I hear whisper in the village about Judy and Manuel, but I didn't make much of it because in this place news, especially news that is not true, travel faster than when people beating African drum. Still, I wanted to talk to Judy. Tell her to watch herself. How you see that man eye long as snake belly so his mind narrow.

'What you mean about Manuel and Judy? I didn't know they in anyting.' I said kind of ieymaetae. 'She better watch sheself you know.'

'Miss Effie, I don't know. I don't know what's going on. Judy tell me she don't want anything to do with the man but he won't leave her alone. I think he drinking too much of Joyce souse water; all that pepper and cucumber water building up in his back. Joyce souse water and Gemma Guinness punch. He better don't let Mammy hear that stupidness because when she finish with him all the water drain out of his back that Gemma don't have any use for him wedding coming up or no wedding.'

Rita will have nineteen in January but the things she say like she already seen the world. I looked at her and laughed. 'Bunjay oye, Rita you is something oui. Whey you does get these thing you does say dey. Anyway, talking about souse and Guinness punch you going to Brian's christening fête by the river on Sunday?'

'Aaaaye. How you mean if I going and I is the baby Godmother.'

Rita stopped sweeping and came into my yard and sat on the stone under the clothes line just over the little drain that run between the two houses. 'I just hope Brian don't ask Henry to buy goat for him,' she started to laugh, first a giggle then in fits, holding her belly as if keeping it in place.

I looked at the girl, her face creased. Water streaking down her face. If anyone came into the yard they'd think that she was either crying or the early morning started burning her skull. I couldn't help but start to laugh as well. Not so much at Rita laughing, but remembering why she was laughing.

'Chupes,' I said, 'Henry too damn stupid. Too stupid and thief.'

'Stupid! I think he made the white rum soak in his

head, soak straight into his brain, if he had any in his head to begin with. How on earth you expect to thief people goat to sell to police man to make fête, eh! You don't see something was wrong with the man in his head.'

'Perhaps was too much bad food he eat. I don't know what kind of thief is that. Henry hear the police and them making fête and they want a goat. See the old lady one goat tie behind her house. Go and offer to sell goat to policeman. They thinking Henry had goat in the bush, gave him the money. And he playing so smart said he would clean and season the meat and bring it ready to cook.'

'Smart he playing saying he going to clean the meat. When he clean it no body could see the skin.'

'Girl, old people always say "man work, God struck". If he didn't cut his foot when he went to cut up the meat he might of got away with it. Anyway, Brian uncle in Prospect is bringing the goat so we don't have to worry.'

'I wonder who Brian getting to help his wife prepare the things. I'm not sure his wife could manage by herself. The family must be coming from Prospect and Mamalaan – they'll help.'

The sun was not well over the mountain. The heat began to rise. The place dry as if no rain fall last night. Rita got off the stone and carry on sweeping as I turned to go back in the kitchen. The same time Judy came from their kitchen towards the back of the house.

'Marning Miss Effie,' she said.

'Marning Judy. What happening girl?'

'I dey so so nuh. I just come to ask Rita if she want fry saltfish or saltfish souse. Eh Rita,' she turned to her sister.

'You frying bakes?' Rita asked. 'If you frying bakes make some fry saltfish.'

As the word fry saltfish come out of Judy mouth my

mind drifted to the girls' grandmother, Miss Etta. I could almost smell her saltfish frying. One thing I must say Judy make a fry saltfish just like her grandmother used to. Miss Etta had a special way of mixing the flour. When she mixed that flour and season it with the onion, thyme, pepper, sieve, then wash the saltfish she had soaking or sometimes she give it a little boil up, mash it up fine fine between her fingers before putting in the flour and mixing it up, she make sure it's not too soft or stiff, it must drop in the oil by spoonful. When she fry that brown and crispy you could smell it all the way down in the foreroad, especially if she frying it in coconut oil. That woman had a sweet mouth, not just the fry saltfish; when she used to make the sugar cake and coconut turnover was the same thing. In the morning she in the bay selling saltfish and bakes to the men and them pulling the net, by twelve o'clock she in the school gap with a glass case of sugar cake and sometimes plum stew waiting for the school children. When the old lady died her daughter – that's Rita and Judy mother – continued with the selling but it wasn't really her thing, she preferred to do her sewing. Looking out over the hill I could almost see the old lady, sitting under the plum tree.

'Judy how you come asking about fry saltfish this Thursday morning eh?' The sharpness in Rita's voice bought me back to the present. Her voice had that what-is-going-on sound. Judy's lips twitched. I looked from one sister to the other; let out a deep breath. Judy better watch herself, I thought to myself.

'Aaye Rita what you mean if I awright? What you see do me eh.' Rita cut her eyes at her sister.

'So Judy you going in christening Sunday?' I asked, more for something to say than anything else.

'Nuh, I can't go you know. I going in St David with the Church young people group. We will be having our own fête there. You know every year we visit each other. We going by them Sunday coming; you remember they came by us in August. Last year when we went was something. You know we always put ourselves out when we have visitors to make sure they have plenty to eat and drink – last year when we went to St David you'd think was the whole island coming. We were suppose to spend most of our time praying and singing. I can't remember much about the prayers but the food, yes. Miss Esther, that's the St David lady that arrange everything, she said the church was too small so they hold the day in the big school; turn one class room into a church to prayer. It was better because the boys had the big playground to play cricket, then we had the concert in the big hall then the dance afterwards. Then there's that big open room with the kitchen on one side and the rest is eating space. It was really nice and the food – Lawd Miss Effie you should of seen the food that those people spread out for us. The whole of one side was tables with drinks, and I mean drinks, not white rum, because you know that church people like no strong liquor. Mind you, I'm sure they had it in secret. Anyway there was sorrel, gingerbeer, sweet drinks, mauby and the rum punch for big people. They call it rum punch but was more fruit than rum. I think they just called it rum punch because it sounded better. Then on one side was a table with the sweet things – sugar cake, fudge, ginger cake, coconut cake, turnover – all kind of things. Then on another side the real food – chicken rice, rice and pease, cookup chicken, goat stew, saltfish souse and bread, provision, fry fish, all kind of things; they even had baskets of mango, sugar apple and plums.

'Miss Effie, I eat that day – I eat and drink. The drink was there like water, but I didn't touch the mauby it's too bitter. I can't drink that thing no matter how much ice I put in it. We really had a good time.'

'So you leaving Brian christening to go to St David eh.' I said when I got the chance to say a word.

'She better don't come back with puff belly,' Rita reminded her sister. 'Miss Effie, when this girl came back last year she had a bag with potato pudding and gingerbread. She even bring back a little of asham. I never hear people having asham in fête. And this girl so greedy she couldn't leave anything. She come home saying she belly hurting ah fus she eat. All night she in the latrine.'

'Aye Rita,' Judy shouted. 'You have to shame me so? Let out me business.'

'After you too greedy, because food on the table don't mean you have to bust your belly. Food not running away – greedy you greedy.'

I looked across the yards from one sister to the other and laughed.

'Well,' I said, 'I know that people quarrel for food not fight about food, and food you eat since last year.'

Just then Ringo started whinging again, whinging and sort of play crying. I looked towards the gap just as my son Cecil cross the piece of plank over the drain leading to our yard.

'Aye Cecil you come out in the garden early?' Rita called to him.

'He going in town this morning before he go in the garage,' I informed Rita. I turned to Cecil as he climbed steps to the kitchen front door. He put down the bag he was carrying, sat down and began fanning himself. 'You awright?' I asked him.

'Yes ma'am. I just tired. The sun not up good yet it feel like is front hell gate and so it make you tired quick.'

I left the girls and went to the kitchen.

'What you get?' I asked opening the bag.

'I dig up some dasheen; they riping already, bursting the ground and I pick some pigeon pease. The piece of potato in the corner by the ravine boundary with Mr George ready to dig, all the vine drying up.'

I poured what was in the bag on to the large garden tray. 'You had time to pick pease as well, and they well full.' Pop, I snapped a pease pod between my fingers. 'I think I'll make some pease soup tonight. There's a piece of salt pork in there from last week, I'll use it up. If I have time later I'll go over the river by Miss Melda for two coconut.'

'I could make up a load for the marketing board tomorrow,' Cecil said. 'Some pease, a few pounds of dasheen, and I notice one or two ripe pumpkin under the mandarin tree by the dwarf coconut tree. I could either sell them to the marketing board or dig some potatoes put with and go in town Saturday morning. What you think ma?'

'You think you'll be able to manage the market Saturday morning? I thought you going to Grenville to help your uncle sort the bananas for shipment? Don't worry about going in town. I'll go up in the garden in the morning to help you get some things for the marketing board and I could sell some by the road. People always love your potato and dasheen; they say it nice and dry. If we had enough pease here I could of asked Joyce to sell some for us – she going in the market today.'

'Joyce going in town today. What she get to sell?' Cecil was surprised.

'She send Junny for callaloo already this morning. Junny say the mother wanted the callaloo to go with coo-coo and fish. The child say Joyce going in today sell. I think she followed Mr Mason in the estate yesterday for orange and mandarin.'

'Perhaps. To tell you the truth ma I don't really want to give my things to Joyce. She have too much sweet mouth. She taking the things selling them and want to give you next to nothing.' Cecil's jaw twitched. I was sure I heard his teeth grinding.

'Eem.' I cleared my throat. I don't know what it is, but Cecil and Joyce eyes could never meet.

'When I going in the garden tomorrow I going to ask Rita to come with me if she not doing anything. She could help me pick the pease and help me bring down the other load,' I said as I set out some bully bakes, saltfish souse and a cup of Milo for Cecil.

'That's awright,' Cecil said, 'she could get some mango. The big 'tin' mango in the middle by the cane stool start to ripe.'

I opened the backroom kitchen window and called to Rita.

'Yes Miss Effie,' she answered.

'What you doing tomorrow morning? I want to run up in the garden for some provision. You want to come for some pease for your mother?'

'If she not coming I could come with you,' Judy shouted from the kitchen. 'Mammy was trying to get two pounds of pease from McDowell. We didn't know yours was ready. Aaaye Cecil you in business man.'

'Is awright Jude I'll go with Miss Effie,' Rita called out. 'So Miss Effie if the pease riping you won't want any callaloo for Sunday, you could sell more. I know my aunt up the road will want hers as usual.'

'Cecil bring down some pease. I thinking about making some pease soup tonight, and pick some more for rice and pease on Sunday when my brother's two daughters, Marcelle and Ruth, coming down. They love rice and pease especially the pigeon pease. How Marcelle love the rice and pease so she love dasheen. Just boil it and if you have some fry jacks she in heaven. She'll eat a plate full then drink water.'

'Marcelle and Cecil not family for nothing,' Rita joked, 'how she love the dasheen so Cecil like breadfruit especially in oil down.'

'Bunjay girl! You have to scandal my name so, eh?' Cecil shouted to Rita. 'You know is not just the breadfruit in the coconut oil I like. Is how my mother cook it with the pepper and salt pork and well steam down.'

Rita by this time had finished sweeping and was standing on the step leading to upstairs their house. 'If you cooking rice and pease on Sunday Miss Effie don't forget to leave my share for me.'

Judy pushed her head out of an upstairs window, 'Aaye aaye I thought you going in christening Sunday, how come you want Miss Effie to leave food for you, eh Rita?'

'Miss Effie don't bother with this girl eh – don't bother with her at all at all, she too farse. When you cook callaloo soup ent you always leave some for her eh? She too farse.'

Somebody who don't know the girls hearing them would think it's little children quarrelling about food. It's always like that since they born. They'll eat at our house and Cecil eat at theirs. Not so much now as when they were younger. One thing they always have a special meal they love. Like Rita it is rice and pease, and Judy callaloo Soup. Cecil is just the same he love the callaloo soup especially if the dumpling mix. He don't really like plain flour dumpling, he prefers either corn flour or cassava in it. I must remember to root a manioc stool tomorrow for some cassava to put in the dumpling. Cecil prefer the flour mix just as he don't really like the plain rice; he say it does give him wind.

'Rita tomorrow please God when we go in the garden remind me to root up a manioc tree eh.'

'Yes Miss Effie. You making starch?'

'No, not really for starch. I want some cassava to put in the flour to make the dumpling and some to make some farina.'

'Bunjay Miss Effie you is something with you food oui.'

'Aaaaye how you mean,' Cecil put in, 'my mother have

to look after me you know.'

'And you like you dumpling,' Judy teased, 'especially cassava dumpling in the callaloo.'

'What you like most Cecil, the manioc or corn flour dumpling?' Rita continued teasing.

'Look girl don't fret me eh. Mind you business. I work hard and I like my food. I don't see anything wrong with that – don't fret me eh.' Cecil pretended to be vex with the girls. They know he only joking. They are accustomed to each other. In a way he is like a brother to them and they like the sister he don't have nearby.

'You like you food especially Miss Effie dumpling, eh Cecs,' Judy continued.

'Judy, saye saye, if he like my dumpling,' I joined in. 'The last time Marcelle came down she cooked dinner and she made dumpling. Girl as soon as the man put his teeth on the flour he complained is not his mother made the dumpling.'

'So Cecil if I make dumpling for Miss Effie you'll know the difference eh?' Rita asked.

'How you mean? Aye aye. My mother hand is special – you know that. That's why when she cook rice and pease or callaloo soup she have to leave a share for you and Judy.'

'Is true you know – is true,' Judy agreed. 'Miss Effie callaloo soup sweet for so – with the salt beef or pig snout and those stiff little dumpling going 'keeeks' when you bite them ... woy o yoye.'

'Callaloo soup eh ... hot and nice,' Rita joined in, 'with some eddoes and a nice piece of St Vincent yam.'

'Yeh with salt beef and corn flour or even cassava dumpling,' Cecil echoed, 'woye o yoye.'

Breathtaking Ignorance

Val McDermid

Every caterer's nightmare. The choking customer, collapsed on the floor gasping for breath. I'd already hurtled through from the kitchen as soon as I heard the coughing and spluttering, and I made it to his side just as he slumped to the floor like a Bonfire Night guy, legs splayed, head lolling, eyes popping.

The boardroom crowd were keeping their distance, remembering all the strictures they'd ever heard about giving people air. There was a nervous hush, the only sounds the croaking gasps of the man on the floor. I knew exactly who he was. Brian Bayley, chief legal executive of Kaymen Merchant Bank. But that didn't stop me kneeling down beside him and dragging him into a sitting position so I could perform the Heimlich manoeuvre. That's one of the many fascinating things you learn at catering college. You encircle the victim with your arms, hug them tightly and sharply, forcing the air out of their lungs, which in turn frees whatever is blocking their windpipe. The downside is that somebody usually ends up covered in sick.

Bayley was bright scarlet by now, his lips turning an ominous blue. I got my arms round him, smelling the sweat that mingled with his expensive cologne. I contracted my arms, forcing his ribs inward. Nothing happened. His gasping sounded more frantic, less effective.

'I'll call an ambulance, Meg,' John Collings said desperately, moving towards the boardroom phone. He'd organised this lunch, and I could see this was the last contract for a directors' thrash that I'd be getting from him.

I tried the manoeuvre again. This time, Bayley slumped heavily against me. The heaving in his chest seemed to have stopped. 'Oh my God,' I said. 'He's stopped breathing.'

A couple of the other guests moved forward and gingerly pulled Bayley's still body away from me. I freed my skirt from under him and crawled round him on my knees, saying, 'Quick, the kiss of life.' Out of the corner of my eye, I could see John slam the phone down. In the corner behind him, Tessa, the waitress who'd served him was weeping quietly.

John's chief accountant had taken on the unenviable task of mouth-to-mouth resuscitation. Somehow, I knew he was wasting his time. I leaned back on my heels, muttering, 'I don't understand it. I just don't understand it.'

The ambulance crew arrived within five minutes and clamped an oxygen mask over his face. They strapped Bayley to a stretcher and I followed them down the corridor and into the lift. David Bromley, Bayley's deputy, climbed into the ambulance alongside me, looking questioningly at me.

'It was my food he was eating,' I said defensively. 'I want to make sure he's all right.'

'Looks a bit late for that,' he said. He didn't sound full of regrets.

At the hospital, David and I found a quiet corner near the WRVS coffee stall. I stared glumly at the floor and said softly, 'He didn't look like he was going to pull through.'

'No,' David agreed with a note almost of relish in his voice.

'You don't sound too upset,' I hazarded.

'That obvious, is it?' he asked pleasantly. 'No I'm not upset. The guy is a complete shit. He's a tyrant at the office, and at home too, from what I can gather. He says jump, the only question you're allowed to ask is, how high. He goes through secretaries like other people go through rolls of Sellotape.'

'Oh God,' I groaned. 'So if he recovers, he'll probably sue me for negligence.'

'I doubt he'd have a case – his own greed was too much of a contributory factor. I saw him stuffing down those chicken canapés like there was no tomorrow,' David consoled me.

Before we could say more, a weary-looking woman in a white coat approached. 'Are you the two people who came in the ambulance with –' she checked her clipboard. 'Brian Bayley?' We nodded. 'Are you related to Mr Bayley?'

We shook our heads. 'I'm a colleague,' David said.

'And I catered the lunch where Mr Bayley had his choking fit,' I revealed.

The doctor nodded. 'Can you tell me what Mr Bayley had to eat?'

'Just some canapés. That's all we'd served by then,' I said defensively.

'And what exactly was in the canapés?'

'There were two sorts,' I explained. 'Chicken or smoked salmon and lobster.'

'Brian was eating the chicken ones,' David added helpfully.

The doctor looked slightly puzzled. 'Are you sure?'

'Of course I'm sure. He never touched fish,' David added. 'He wouldn't even have it on the menu if we were hosting a function.'

'Look,' I said. 'What exactly is the problem here?'

The doctor sighed. 'Mr Bayley has died, apparently as the result of going into anaphylactic shock.' We must both have looked bewildered, for she went on to explain. 'A profound allergic reaction. Essentially, the pathways in his respiratory tract just closed up. He couldn't physically get air into his lungs, so he asphyxiated. I've never heard of it being brought on by chicken, though. The most common cause is an allergic reaction to a bee sting,' she added thoughtfully.

'I know he was allergic to shellfish,' David offered. 'That's why he had this thing about not serving fish.'

'Oh my God,' I wailed. 'The lobster!' They both stared at me. 'I ground up the lobster shells into powder and mixed them with mayonnaise for the fish canapés. The mayo for the chicken ones had grilled red peppers mixed into it. They both looked the same. Surely there coudn't have been a mix-up in the kitchen?' I covered my face with my hands as I realised what I'd done.

Of course, they both fussed over me and insisted it wasn't my fault. I pulled myself together after a few minutes, then the doctor asked David about Bayley's next of kin. 'His wife's called Alexandra,' he told her, and recited their home number.

How did I know it was their home number? Oh, didn't I mention that Alexandra and I have been lovers for just over a year now? And that Brian was adamant that if she left him, he'd make sure she left without a penny from him? And, more importantly, that she'd never see her children again?

I just hope the mix-up with the mayo won't hurt my reputation for gourmet boardroom food too much.

From Anita and Me

Meera Syal

'Anita's mom has run away,' I said. Mama and papa stared at me sharply.

'Meena, if you are lying again ...'

'She left a note and went off with a butcher. Anita was dead upset, crying and everything. She did not know what she was saying, I reckon ...' Well, I would have believed it.

Mama sat down heavily on one of the high backed chairs at the table. 'That poor poor girl,' she said softly. 'She did not deserve this ...'

Papa pulled me, gently now, to his side and enquired, 'Who is looking after her?'

'Them,' interjected mama. 'She has a little sister – Tina?'

'Tracey,' I said, in the tone of a funeral director discussing casket size.

Mama continued, 'I mean, they need to eat, the house

needs keeping, the father works, what will happen?' Mama was worrying weeks ahead on their behalf, she was already on her feet. 'I'm going to chat with Mrs Worrall, maybe we can set up some kind of rota ...'

Papa raised his hand, 'Daljit, no. Sit a minute.'

Mama hesitated. Nanima meanwhile was squirming with curiosity, Punjabi machine-gunned round our heads whilst mama and papa tried to continue the conversation. '*Ik minute, mataji,*' papa reassured her. 'Daljit, we can't interfere ... '

'Oh my God, that is such an English thing to say! You have been living here too long! There are little children involved.'

'I know that,' papa continued. 'But we are not their family. They would see it as ... well, rude. Patronising even. If they ask for help, that is a different matter, but we can't just take over the way we do with our friends. 'Think about it please. They have their pride.'

Mama stood in the doorway, chewing her lip. She suddenly scooped up Sunil and smothered him with passionate kisses whilst he protested loudly. 'You are still my baby, you naughty *munda*! Keep still!'

Nanima was getting annoyed now, and rattled off another loud enquiry to mama who replied back in a suitably scandalised tone. Nanima understood, shook her head and carefully screwed a forefinger into her temple, apeing what I had taught her months back. 'Meena,' papa said, stroking my neck. 'Ask Anita if she wants to come and eat with us. Any time. And her sister. Don't force her though. She might want to spend some time with her daddy right now ...'

'Can I come tonight?' said Anita when I knocked at her back gate half an hour later.

Anita turned up alone and empty-handed, wearing her

new school jumper with a pair of flared jeans. 'Tracey didn't want to come,' was the first thing she said to my parents who stood by the door, as they did for all our visitors, ready to take her coat. 'Oh, that's okay, darling,' said mama, ushering her in and waving at papa to remove one of the place settings from the dining table. I had insisted that we sit at the table, something we never did with Indian guests since we usually ate in shifts. But tonight, I had set the table myself; even putting Sunil's high chair next to mama's place, and told her, 'Don't just run to and from the kitchen burning your fingers like you normally do. I want us to sit and talk, you know, like you're supposed to do at dinners.' I could have asked mama to tap-dance on top of the telly wearing false boobs and playing the spoons and she might have considered it, so anxious was she to mop the brow of our motherless guest.

I knew Anita well enough not to expect a great display of mourning, but even I was surprised by her complete lack of emotion, or indeed, social graces. She watched *Top of the Pops* through all papa's attempts to engage her in friendly chitchat, during which he steered clear of anything that might possibly be connected with Mothers. 'So Anita ... um, how's school?' Anita grunted and turned up the volume control, shifting away from Sunil who was edging towards her holding the edge of the sofa, desperate to make friends with this new face. 'Your par ... your father, does he take you or do you go by bus?' Anita stifled a yawn and reached for another crisp from our nick-nacks bowl, as mama called it, which was now almost empty.

Mama had gone to the trouble of preparing two menus, which was fortunate considering Anita's reaction when the serving dishes of various curries were placed in front of her. 'What's that!' she demanded, as if confronted with a festering sheep's head on a platter. 'Oh that's mattar-paneer,' mama said proudly, always happy to educate the sad English palate. 'A sort of Indian cheese, and these are peas with it, of course ... '

'Cheese and peas?' said Anita faintly. 'Together?'

'Well,' mama went on hurriedly. 'This is chicken curry ... You have had chicken before, haven't you?'

'What's that stuff round it?'

'Um, just gravy, you know, tomatoes, onions, garlic ...' Mama was losing confidence now, she trailed off as she picked up Anita's increasing panic.

'Chicken with tomatoes? What's garlic?'

'Don't you worry!' papa interjected heartily, fearing a culinary cat fight was about to shatter his fragile peace. 'We've also got fishfingers and chips. Is tomato sauce too dangerous for you?'

Anita's relief made her oblivious to his attempt at a joke. She simply picked up her knife and fork and rested her elbows on the table, waiting to be served with something she could recognise. 'I'll have fishfingers, mum! Um, please!' I called out after her. I could tell from the set of mama's back that her charity was wearing a little thin. Although I had yet to cast Anita in the mould of one of the Rainbow orphan kids, I did wonder if food was a problem at her house after seeing her eat. Any romantic idea I had about witty stories over the dinner table disappeared when Anita made a fortress of her arms and chewed stolidly behind it, daring anyone to approach and disturb her concentration or risk losing an eye if they attempted to steal a chip. She looked up only twice, once when my parents began eating, as always, with their fingers, using their chapatti as scoops to ferry the banquet of curries into their mouths.

Anita stopped in mid-chew, looking from her knife and fork to mama and papa's fingers with faint disgust, apparently unaware that all of us had a great view of a lump of half masticated fishfinger sitting on her tongue. It had never occurred to me that this would be a moment of controversy, it had never occurred to me because I had never eaten Indian food in the presence of a white person before. In fact, I only then realised that Anita Rutter was the first non-relative to sit and break bread with us, and the same thought had just hit my parents, who had gradually slowed down their eating and were eyeing a nearby box of paper hankies with longing. I snapped to attention, I would not have Anita play the same games with my parents that had made me dizzy and confused. The girl had not even said a simple thank you yet. 'We always eat our food with our fingers,' I said loudly to Anita. 'Like in all the top restaurants. Bet you didn't know that, did you?' For the first time that I could remember, my parents caught a lie flying out of my mouth and threw it right back at me with a cheer. Mama and papa both looked at their plates, their mouths twitching, until Sunil broke the moment by emptying his plate of rice over his head. Nanima lumbered into action with the box of tissues, pushing past Anita clumsily and leaning over her to reach Sunil with no regard to English body language rules.

In fact, whilst my parents did their dance of welcome around Anita all evening, my Nanima remained singularly uninvolved and unimpressed. She stood in front of the television, apparently unaware of Anita's sighs and craning neck, she slumped next to her on the settee, making Anita sink into the cushions, and gradually edged towards her until she gave up and moved to the floor, allowing Nanima to lie at full stretch, massaging her feet which she occasionally waved under Anita's nose, making her jump and hold her breath. I only began to suspect her exaggerated old lady behaviour was perhaps deliberate when she made Anita look up for the second time from her food, by letting fly the longest, loudest burp I had ever had the privilege to witness. I swear Anita's blonde bangs flew up in protest against the velocity, and even mama uttered an involuntary '*Hai Ram*, mama!'

Anita looked like she was waiting for an apology, so papa hurriedly chipped in with 'We often take a good burp as a sign of a good meal, Anita. Also, you know old ladies are a bit freer with their ... um ... expressions. Does your granny suffer in this manner?'

Anita thought for a moment and said carefully, 'Me dad's mom died ages ago. Mom's mom used to leave her toenail clippings in our plant pots though.'

I sighed with relief, now we were equal, and just to prove it, Anita finished her last chip, steeled herself and finally did thank my parents with a window-shattering belch. Mama did not bat an eyelid. 'My pleasure, darling,' she replied.

From *Anita and Me*, published by Flamingo

Break All the Rules

Linda Wilkinson

'It's not like one of those television ads you know. Boil-in-the-bag, open a packet stuff, I've got to get it right.'

'But honestly, nobody but you will know whether it's right, or not. I've never eaten it and I doubt that either Helen or Chris will ever have heard of it.'

I looked down at the grey, slimy skin and white flesh which was flecked with blood, 'What did you say you have with it, the vegetables I mean?'

Sarah turned back from her investigation of the kitchen cupboard and its contents.

'Potatoes.'

'And?'

'No, "and", just potatoes, boiled potatoes.'

I felt an incipient desire for a curry but managed to suppress the impulse to suggest that we have that particular ethnic meal instead of Sarah's own.

'Damn, we've got no all-spice.'

'We've never had any all-spice Sarah, don't lose your temper.'

Sarah's mother, Rebecca, was haltingly, but most definitely, dying from senile dementia. At first she had lost a word here and there, soon the thread of a sentence eluded her, and now, conversations were a jumbled mass of disconnected half-sounds and shrugs. From initial denial, Sarah was battling towards an acceptance that this strong, capable woman, her mother, was now an imbecilic wreck. The progress of the disease had galvanised Sarah into a reinvestigation of her roots, not least of which were her culinary roots. Both her mother and grandmother, so she told me, had held the secret for preparing the best salt beef and conger eel that Sarah had ever tasted. Ingénue that I was, I had expressed a desire to taste these delights and, even more foolishly, had agreed that she could cook one of them for our next dinner party. Salt beef, for very obvious health reasons, never made it past the starting post, but fish, well it was a wholesome meal, wasn't it?

'I've got to have some all-spice, not the powdered stuff but the whole seeds.'

'Do you think that we should freeze this batch of fish, just for us, and have something else this evening?'

Her eyes narrowed and filled with tears, 'I knew you'd do this.'

'Well, I have to admit, it looks unappetising in the extreme. I thought you'd cook it in tomatoes and garlic or something, but just boiled fish and boiled potatoes hardly grabs me.'

She opened her mouth to proclaim the lack of garlic in East London in the nineteenth century. I had heard it all before, the mantra of her past, her family's past, but this was different; the food, this food, signified her way of coping with what was happening to her mother. The continuity of tradition had, for this moment in time, become focused on the preparation of conger eel and parsley sauce. I acquiesced, 'I'll get some all-spice, do you need anything else?'

'Parsley, more parsley.'

Sarah seemed already to have liberated Sainsbury's of its whole stock of parsley, I opened my mouth to comment, but thought better of it.

It was some time later that I returned, having discovered that all-spice, whole all-spice, was not a common commodity. Sarah was on the phone to Rebecca. Their phone conversations were painful in the extreme, the disconnections within Rebecca's mind required the ingenuity of a mind-reader to unravel. Finally, Sarah put down the telephone. She looked exhausted.

'I can't remember how to cook it, and she can't tell me.'

I had a deep, and as it transpired well-founded, suspicion that Sarah had never, ever, cooked either of the traditional delights she so loved to eat. 'Does she still know how to cook it?'

'Yes, but I can't get it out of her.'

I could feel her pain. 'Listen, why don't I pick her up, she could have dinner with us, Helen and Chris won't mind – she'll go to bed long before we get into dessert.'

'But she can't say anything; she'll just sit there like a zombie.'

It really didn't matter to me if Rebecca took off all her clothes and danced around the kitchen incanting witchcraft, as long as Sarah cheered up. 'The options are, freeze the fish and we get a takeaway, or I go get mother ... '

'Phone her and tell her I'm on my way. You start chopping that mountain of parsley.'

Rebecca stood outside the block of flats in which, miraculously, she continued to live alone. Clutching the supermarket plastic bag which she had adopted as her overnight case, she looked like a faded, but still beautiful, version of Sarah. Her eyes, which when I had first met her ten years previously, had danced and sparkled with life and fun, now looked flat, lifeless.

The technique I used to cope with her, was to blather on about anything and nothing. Occasionally she interjected with an ill-timed, 'Really, oh you don't say,' or some such expression. Today, however, she was fired up with the subject of fish and its cooking. Somewhere in the mess of her mind lived the recipe which Sarah had never learned.

'Has, has she got the Cccc?' She staggered and searched for the word.

'Conger eel?' I asked.

She nodded

Not being able to face the onslaught of a protracted memory session, I filled in the missing links, 'She's got the fish, parsley, lots of parsley, all-spice, potatoes, that's all isn't it?'

She shook her head and I groaned inwardly.

'No vinegar, you got vinegar?'

I nodded.

'Good,' she stammered. 'And, the white stuff?'

This was always the clincher, the start of a twenty questions session. Did she mean cocaine? I wanted to ask, but no, I was kind and restricted myself to the kitchen.

'Salt?'

No.

'Tea towels?'

No.

'Kitchen roll?'

No.

'Was it liquid?'

No.

'What do you do with it?'

The answer left me no wiser, 'You wait until it's ready then put it in.'

I told her to wait until she could show Sarah as I wanted to concentrate on my driving and, after a few moments she was sound asleep.

'The white stuff? Oh, that's cornflour.' Sarah informed me while mother was in the toilet. 'You have to thicken up the stock before you cook the fish.'

'Surely after.'

'No, why?'

Well, it did contravene every theory of cuisine that I had ever encountered, but one can always learn so I decided not to pursue that line of questioning any further, adopting a wait-and-see strategy.

I suspected that Sarah and Rebecca had always communicated in a wordless fashion, as there was no friction involved in the silent kitchen etiquette which unfolded before my eyes. I sat, glass of wine in hand, wondering if I should warn our guests to have a snack before they came, just in case dinner was inedible. The first hurdle was over, Rebecca approved of Sarah's choice of fish, it was, apparently, fresh and fairly bone free. She chopped even more of the parsley, peeled the potatoes, measured out three heaped spoonfuls of cornflour, then sat down with an air of resignation.

I looked at Sarah questioningly.

'Mum, do you want to start cooking?' she asked.

Rebecca shook her head, 'Fresh, best fresh.'

'But how long will it take to cook?' I had to ask, the fish looked pretty thick to me.

Rebecca looked at the clock. 'Once all the way round,' she said.

'An hour,' Sarah translated.

I looked at her in panic, our guests were due in less than

half an hour – would the meal be both inedible, and served at midnight? She firmly ignored my look and poured her mother a glass of Guinness.

Helen and Chris arrived, we'd finished the hors-d'oeuvre and all was well, or so I thought, when Sarah emerged from the kitchen. 'She wants you in there, not me.'

'But why?'

'I don't know, she's in one of her moods. Just write it all down for me.'

'I can't read her mind like you.'

'Try, she won't budge.'

We smiled at our indulgent guests, who in response to our explanation of the situation proclaimed that they loved fish, in any guise, and switched places.

Rebecca was humming under her breath and stirring a voluptuously boiling pot of water which had parsley and all-spice bobbing on its surface, another pot stood simmering in wait for the potatoes.

'How long?' she asked pointing at the timer which Sarah must have set.

'Two minutes.'

She agreed and picked up the cup which contained the cornflour, 'This white stuff,' she said, 'Just right, or the rest no good, understand?'

I nodded as she mixed the cornflour with cold water and handed me the cup.

'You ... '

She ran out of words, but indicated that I should pour the cornflour into the water and stir.

'It changes,' she said. I must have looked blank for she took the spoon off me, 'Feel, it changes.'

I guessed that I was waiting for the change in viscosity which would herald the fact that the fish should go into the water. I was sure that the resultant glutinous mass would congeal into concrete at the bottom of the pot, but it was too late now.

She gave me back the spoon, 'Now, put – ' She indicated the fish and the potatoes. I put them into their respective pots as she adjusted the level of boiling.

'How long?' I asked, pointing at the timer. She drew a half circle with her finger on the kitchen bench, 'Half an hour?' I asked, she nodded.

I moved towards the door, thinking that I would reclaim the lounge and sanity, but she grabbed my arm. 'Me, the way I am,' she pointed to her head, 'Sarah, she – ' The word would not come, as so often it wouldn't.

I sat her down at the kitchen table. 'Take your time Rebecca, you'll remember.'

'Sarah, she, it hurts?'

'Of course, she hates seeing you like this.'

'Me too,' she grinned. 'But I know, I see, I know, just can't say. The fish, why?'

I shrugged, hoping to escape, hoping that she would forget, but she held on tightly to the thread.

'She never, before,' she pointed at the bubbling pots, 'Never before.'

'I guessed she had never cooked it.'

'No, never. Now she thinks I.'

She made a motion with her hands which I took to mean that soon she, Rebecca, would be gone. I swallowed hard, it was so difficult to know what she understood, what she could understand. Sarah was grieving now, more surely than she would when it was finally over. Death, her mother's death, would be a release from the painful, constant, disintegration being enacted before her eyes.

'I don't really understand it. She wants to communicate with you and somehow the food, the food that you and your mother cooked, has become some kind of symbol.'

She stood to stir the bubbling pot, taking a small

amount of the stock on a spoon she cooled, then tasted it. She added a little more salt, 'Sarah, she's sad, so sad. No need, no need. I remember, it was good, you tell her.'

'Why don't you talk to her?'

She smiled, indulgently, suddenly it was I who didn't understand. 'No, she wants what isn't, what was, you see it for how it is.'

'But surely, at least, you should teach her how to cook this?' I indicated the array before me.

She shook her head and laughed, 'You know, I can't say, but you know.'

Indeed I did. Sarah had the most advanced facility for remembering only the things she wanted to, and in the order she wanted to. I had developed a profound love-hate relationship with her accumulated mis-memory, which had resulted in some of the worst meals and holidays I could ever have imagined.

Rebecca patted my hands. 'You remember for her, you; the right way, the fish, the white stuff, remember, feel it.' She made a stirring motion with her hand.

'Yes, I'll remember.'

The kitchen began to fill with a hot, spicy aroma. Rebecca smiled again, the fish was obviously behaving itself.

When the fish was finally cooked, neither Sarah nor her mother would allow me to trim away the grey skin, or chop into more elegantly, aesthetically pleasing shapes. The huge chunks of white flesh, surrounded by their slightly oily and green tinged sauce, were proclaimed cooked to perfection and delivered to our less than enthusiastic guests, intact.

With trepidation I tasted the sauce, it was light and tasted very subtly of spice and parsley, the fish had infused a marvellous flavour into the slightly thickened broth. Even Helen and Chris — to my surprise — declared the meal a triumph.

We looked on, bemused, as Sarah and Rebecca poured huge volumes of brown vinegar into this delicious brew.

'Why did you do that?' I asked, horrified.

'You must.' Rebecca was adamant, 'Taste.' She held a spoonful out for me.

'It obscures the flavours, it's delicious without vinegar. Why bother to do all that with the cornflour and spices if you pour vinegar in it, you may as well not bother?'

'Nan always put vinegar in, it's part of the recipe, isn't that right Mum?'

Rebecca studied me for a moment, then pointed to my plate. I held a spoonful out to her, she tasted it, mulling over the flavours.

'Good, but I like vinegar,' she ate with gusto.

Sarah grinned over at me, 'Have you learnt how to cook it?'

I made a stirring motion with my hand. 'Yes, all you have to do is break all the rules.'

Contributors' Notes

Maya Angelou was born in 1928 in St Louis, Missouri. After the break-up of her parents' marriage she and her brother Bailey went to live with their grandmother, whose general store was the centre of life for the black community in Stamps, Arkansas. At sixteen, having just graduated from school, Maya gave birth to her son, Guy.

In the years that followed she was a waitress, singer, actress, dancer, black activist, editor, as well as mother. In her twenties she toured Europe and Africa in *Porgy and Bess*. Moving to New York, she joined the Harlem Writers' Guild while continuing to earn her living as a nightclub singer and performer in Genet's *The Blacks*. She became involved in black struggles in the 1960s and then spent several years in Ghana as editor of *African Review*.

Maya Angelou's five books of autobiography, *I Know Why the Caged Bird Sings*, *Gather Together In My Name*, *Singin' and Swingin' and Gettin' Merry Like Christmas*, *The Heart of a Woman* and *All God's Children Need Travelling Shoes*, are a testament to the talents and resilience of this extraordinary writer.

Jean Buffong is a Grenadian who has lived in England

since 1962. She is the author of two novels, *Under the Silk Cotton Tree* (The Women's Press, 1992) and *Snowflakes in the Sun* (The Women's Press, 1995); and a novella, *Jump-Up-and-Kiss-Me*, published together with Nellie Payne's *A Grenadian Childhood* in the popular *Jump-Up-and-Kiss-Me: Two Stories from Grenada* (The Women's Press, 1990).

Ana Castillo is an award-winning poet with five collections of poetry, including: *Women are not Roses, My Father Was a Toltec,* and *I Ask the Impossible: New and Collected Poems.* She has published three novels: *So Far from God* (The Women's Press, 1994), *The Mixquiahuala Letters,* which received the American Book Award, and *Sapogonia*; a collection of short stories, *Loverboys*; a children's book, *My Son, My Eagle, My Dove*; and is the author of a book of critical feminist essays, *Massacre of the Dreamers: Essays on Xicanisma.* A native of Chicago, Ana Castillo now makes her home in Albuquerque, New Mexico.

Stevie Davies, who lives near Manchester, is a novelist and literary critic, with an honorary appointment as Senior Research Fellow at Roehampton Institute, London. She lectured at Manchester University from 1971–84, leaving to write full-time. She has published eleven volumes of biography and literary criticism, the most recent being her life of Henry Vaughan (1995) and *Emily Brontë: Heretic* (The Women's Press, 1994).

Her first novel, *Boy Blue* (The Women's Press, 1987), won the Fawcett Book Prize for 1989; *Primavera* (The Women's Press, 1990) confirmed her literary reputation; and her shattering breakthrough book, *Arms and the Girl* (The Women's Press, 1992), received universal acclaim. *Closing the Book* (The Women's Press, 1994) was on the long-list for the Booker Prize in 1994, and the shortlist for the Fawcett Book Prize in 1995. Her most recent novel,

Four Dreamers and Emily, was published by The Women's Press in 1996.

Jyl Lynn Felman is a writer, cultural activist and performance artist. She is an award-winning short story writer whose work appears in newspapers, literary journals and anthologies; and the author of a one-act play, *Voices*. Jyl Lynn Felman is also an attorney, and lectures widely on racism, anti-Semitism, and homophobia.

Ellen Galford was born in New Jersey, USA, but emigrated to Scotland in 1971, and defines herself as an adopted Scot. In 1978 she joined a feminist writers' group working in Edinburgh and Fife, and — with their encouragement — wrote her first novel, *Moll Cutpurse: Her True History.* She is the author of three other novels: *The Fires of Bride* (The Women's Press, 1986), *Queendom Come*, and *The Dyke and the Dybbuk*. She has also contributed to various feminist, and lesbian and gay anthologies, including the short story collection *Girls Next Door* (The Women's Press, 1985). She lives in Edinburgh.

Hiromi Goto was born in 1966 in Japan, and emigrated to Canada at the age of three with her family. After a short time on the West Coast, they moved to southern Alberta. Hiromi graduated with a BA degree in English from the University of Calgary in 1989. Her first novel, *Chorus of Mushrooms* (The Women's Press, 1997), won the Commonwealth Writers' Prize for Best First Book, Canada and the Caribbean Region. She lives in Calgary.

Githa Hariharan was educated in Bombay, Manila and the United States where she also worked in public television. Since 1979, she has worked in Bombay, Madras and New Delhi, first as an editor in a publishing house, then as a freelancer. *The Thousand Faces of Night* (The Women's Press, 1996) won the Commonwealth Writers' Prize for the Best First Novel. Githa Hariharan has also published *The Art of Dying*, a collection of her short stories; another novel, *The Ghosts of Vasu Master*; and edited *A Southern Harvest*, an anthology of short stories. Her stories have appeared in magazines and journals internationally.

Andrea Levy was born in London in 1956 and studied textile and fashion design. She worked for the BBC and the Royal Opera House before becoming a graphic designer. Her first novel, *Every Light in the House Burnin'*, was published in 1994 and her second, *Never Far from Nowhere*, was published in 1996. She has given many readings and her work has also been broadcast on BBC Radio 4. She has also been a judge for the Saga Prize and the New Venture and Pandora awards.

Val McDermid grew up in a Scottish mining community. She worked as a journalist in Scotland for fourteen years, becoming National Bureau Chief of a major national Sunday tabloid. She quit journalism in 1991 and has since become a full-time writer.

Val McDermid is the author of five best-selling Lindsay Gordon mysteries: *Report for Murder, Common Murder, Final Edition, Union Jack* and *Booked for Murder*, all published by The Women's Press; as well as the acclaimed Kate Brannigan mystery series. In 1995 she won the Crime Writers' Association Gold Dagger Award for best crime novel.

Lesléa Newman is a writer and editor with over twenty books to her credit including *Fat Chance* (Livewire Books, The Women's Press, 1996), *SomeBODY To Love: A Guide to Loving the Body You Have, Eating Our Hearts Out: Personal Accounts of Women's Relationships to Food, Every*

Woman's Dream, and *Heather Has Two Mommies*. Her literary awards include a Massachusetts Artists' Foundation Fellowship in Poetry and a *Highlights for Children* Fiction Writing Award. She lives in Massachusetts.

Mei Ng is a writer living in New York.

M Nourbese Philip was born in Tobago in the Caribbean, took her first degree, in Economics, at the University of West Indies, and finished studying in Ontario, Canada. She was a barrister and solicitor from 1975 to 1982. M Nourbese Philip has published three books of poetry, including *She Tries Her Tongue, Her Silence Softly Breaks* (The Women's Press, 1993), and is a contributor to several anthologies. She has also published a Young Adult novel, *Harriet's Daughter*.

Erika Ritter was born in Saskatchewan, Canada. She studied drama at McGill University in Montreal, and earned a Masters degree from the Drama Centre of the University of Toronto in 1970. After teaching for three years, she embarked upon a freelance writing career, combining play-writing, humorous essays, short fiction, radio plays and radio broadcasting.

Erika Ritter's published works include a play, *Automatic Pilot*, as well as two collections of humorous pieces, *Urban Scrawl* and *Ritter in Residence*, and numerous short stories and articles. She has also been a humour columnist and social satirist for newspapers and magazines in Canada, as well as on air for various radio programmes.

Currently, Erika Ritter divides her time between Toronto and Eastern New York State, and has recently completed her first novel.

Michèle Roberts was born in 1949 of a French mother and English father. *A Piece of the Night,* published in 1978, was her début novel, and also the first work of original fiction to be published by The Women's Press. It established Michèle Roberts as a major literary writer, and was followed by *The Visitation* (The Women's Press, 1983). Michèle Roberts is now an established and acclaimed writer of poetry and prose, including her novel, *Daughters of the House*, which was shortlisted for the 1992 Booker Prize and won the WH Smith Literary Award 1993.

Meera Syal, a British-born Indian, is an actress with a number of TV, theatre and film credits, including the screenplay for the film *Bhaji on the Beach*. She has also appeared in *The Real McCoy* and *Have I Got News For You*. Her début novel, *Anita and Me*, was published in 1996.

Kathleen Tyau is a Chinese-Hawaiian woman who grew up in Hawaii, on the island of Oahu. She attended college in the mainland USA, and has worked as a handweaver and legal secretary. She is the author of *A Little Too Much Is Enough* (The Women's Press, 1996), and her short stories have been published widely.

Linda Wilkinson was born in London in 1952. For the majority of her working life she was a scientist in the field of medical research. She has travelled widely and lived, for a while, in Italy where she worked as a waitress serving 200 workers from an industrial plant factory a three-course lunch and wine in forty-five minutes – the quickest way to learn a language she has ever come across! Since 1995 she has been writing creative fiction and is currently writing a stage play. One of her other loves is opera, about which she gave a twenty-minute talk on 'Viva' in their 'how to bluff your way in' slot. In addition she produced the 'Art Show' for Freedom FM radio during their second run in December 1995.